Apple Pie

David Mazzotta

AmErica House
Baltimore

Copyright 1997 by David Mazzotta

All rights reserved. No part of this book may be reproduced in any form without written permission from the publishers, except by a reviewer who may quote brief passages in a review to be printed in a newspaper or magazine.

First printing

ISBN: 1-58851-552-4

PUBLISHED BY AMERICA HOUSE BOOK PUBLISHERS
www.publishamerica.com
Baltimore

Printed in the United States of America

ONE

My name is Alex Kim and I want to get something out of the way before we go one sentence further. I am not Korean. Both my parents are, but not me.

I used to attend the University of Michigan studying aerospace engineering, but even then I was not an Asian whiz kid. My SAT scores were only slightly above average and my grades were equally below. I didn't spend every waking hour studying. I overslept regularly and preferred to play Midnight Frisbee Golf in the Arboretum rather than perform differential Calculus. I've never even been to another country (Windsor, Ontario doesn't count). So whatever impressions you form from my description of my life and myself, remember: I was born in Grosse Pointe, not Seoul. I'm not Korean; I'm American.

A prideful declaration that I am American may seem like a paltry revelation. I can see why you'd think so since in all likelihood you are American and have never thought twice about it, yet I cling to it as the one certainty that came out of the last year of my life. Everything else seems indistinct and chaotic. I sense that I should be able to draw something of metaphysical significance from a frank evaluation of the events, but it all ends up a muddle after about two minutes of thoughtful analysis. Deep thinking on the topic, usually done cloistered in the dark recesses of some overly designed café under the influence of a couple of Ethiopian Hazelnut blends, spins into a swirl of causal loops and deterministic paradoxes in short order. Thus, the book you have in hand. I figure if I can document the events, walk through them in roughly chronological order while maintaining a discrete authorly distance, a theme may arise, something of value that I can work with to better understand why what happened happened.

On the other hand (which I should have amputated), whatever there is to learn from this is only a matter of definition at this point. Such lessons are rarely clearly evident, instead insinuating themselves into your daily life as new instincts to be reacted to as one might thoughtlessly decline candy from a stranger without pausing to assess the philosophical underpinnings of the behavior. By definition, I already react as a man who has experienced what I have experienced. But that's not enough this time. There is simply no way I'm going to have my life turned inside out and not bother to try to figure out why it happened. Was it my fault that I fell for her? Or did my

APPLE PIE

stultifying existence drive me into the arms of cataclysm? And how did I get myself into such an existence to begin with? Am I truly responsible for it all? The path of causality leads back to me, but causality is not control. Did free will lead me here or was my choice limited to the method of my execution? You see what I mean about getting swamped in the core questions of being.

But I digress.

I can, in fact, pinpoint the instant where it all began. As I said, about a year ago. It was a strange sort of snapshot moment, frozen in my subconscious only to periodically reappear in crystalline detail to tease me into pensive, meditative sulks. No, that's too strong—I'm confused and borderline obsessed, but not dour, mopey, or even unhappy as far as I can tell.

I wasn't unhappy back then either. Things seemed to be going pretty much according to plan; a plan I assumed to be mine. There were bumps and turbulence here and there, all negligible in the context of my limited awareness and provincial naivete. I was sharing an apartment with three roommates, the same apartment and roommates as the previous year, and the year before that, and the year before that. We never really fought; we were too superficial to take serious offense at each other. The problem was that I was beginning to realize what my roommates were, gradually, like how you realize that *Saturday Night Live* is not all that funny. They were dweebs. Not plain old dweebs in the sense of nerds in extremis, these were dweebs of such purity and totality they could rightly be called definitive. The Buddhas of dweebhood. Allow me to introduce you.

Peter, dweeb alpha, was a stocky—call it chubby—oaf with a superior attitude. I'm bound to say the guy did do well in school which made him superior in that most superfluous way. He took this circumstance as proof that he was much smarter than anyone who crossed his path, a belief he did not hesitate to express in a very forthright and pompous manner. Naturally, this exceptional intellect lent significance and irrefutability to all his opinions. He would hold forth on why Asimov was better than Bradbury or why Feynmann was smarter than Hawking or why Linux was the only real operating system, that last item being delivered in the form of a sermon. Once he even started in on how male-female relationships were no different among humans than any other species. Like he would know. I was able to put a stop to that by casually mentioning that there were new Pamela Anderson photos posted on the web.

Dweeb beta was a wan, high-waisted pencil neck who had an aversion to washing his hair when he took a shower, which in itself was an exceptional occurrence. His intellect was inconsequential and his social skills had not progressed since potty training. (On two separate occasions I heard him say, in total seriousness, "Shut up, you stupid head.") He had a tendency to snort in reaction to most external stimuli and he was apparently so proud that he had mastered that art of chewing his food that he showed off by keeping his mouth open while doing so. His name was Eustace, pronounced Useless, and as near as I could tell, his only intrinsic value was as an anthropological curiosity. He never got a grade lower than an A-.

Since my knowledge of Greek is spent, dweeb number three, Lenny, was the least offensive of the trio. He listened exclusively to 1970s progressive rock and played air guitar in between breaks from the Sony Playstation. He latched on to that annoying habit of adding hip suffixes to everybody's name, which for a time was a mainstay of bad TV comedy skits. He just never got over it. I disliked it especially because my name doesn't lend itself easily to that practice. Alex-meister and Alex-o-rama just don't cut it. But that was the worst of it; at least he was sanitary. I never saw him open a book, but even he got better grades than I did.

I met this threesome at freshmen orientation shortly after enrolling. We linked up as roommates because we all immediately realized that none of us were axe murderers or prone to any sort of violence nor were we comfortable in the sort of social situations that most people were. In other words, we saw and appreciated our common anxieties and knew that, because of that, we would not judge each other lest we be judged. Also, we were all too anal to be a day late with rent so there was no fear of eviction. It seemed to make sense to stick together rather than risk our fortunes to roommate roulette.

Since we were all majoring in aerospace engineering I had the distinct pleasure of not only living with them, but having them in most of my classes too. Over the years I had gone from accepting them as my clique to being mildly annoyed by their peculiarities to seeing them as a hindrance to a normal life. Let me be more specific, they had come to make my skin crawl with their infantile antics and maladaptive behavior. I can't count how many times I wanted to bellow and rail at their inanities, but bellowing and railing aren't my strong suits.

Besides, I got the impression that they still thought of our little foursome as a kind of fraternity of like-minded (or like-mindless) souls. They were comfortable in the knowledge that they would not be belittled for their social shortcomings and felt as though they were within a fortress of friendship. None of this was ever spoken outright, but it was understood. I was never up to their level of dweebosity, and as such I lent a certain legitimacy to the group. They weren't totally weird because Alex was their friend. If they needed badly for someone to think they were normal they could always arrange for me to be present to show they were really part of humanity. Thoughts like that turned my disgust to pity and I would bite my tongue instead of losing my temper.

Back to the point. If this book were a screenplay, this would be the Fade In. It was late September; senior year having started a couple of weeks earlier. The Dweebs and I were sitting around our hand-me-down circular dining table, studying, as was our habit. We had studied for three hours on Monday and two on Wednesday and Thursday every week for the past three years. I had a reasonable, if uninspiring, social life for the other nights. The Dweebs spent those nights doing an assortment of, well, dweeby things that evolved only slightly over the years. Maybe once or twice a year they did something that required interaction with the outside world, except, of course, for browsing the web.

The idea of three nights a week devoted to study may sound laudable, but it was done as inefficiently as possible. Peter, Useless and I would sit around the table with our books open and converse in a mixture of insult and false insight, with little attention paid to actual schoolwork. Lenny would be wandering about, playing air guitar to Led Zeppelin or Pink Floyd and occasionally chime in with an observation of no consequence. We never bothered to turn the TV off so it was droning on in the background subliminally suggesting we were amidst society.

It was an evening exactly like that when this snapshot kind of moment occurred. For about sixty seconds I could hear none of the bickering or dreadful music. Like a distant object coming into focus, I centered on the TV. On screen was a little Asian girl, possibly Korean, possibly not, no more than seven years old. She didn't smile and never gave more than a one-word answer to any of the condescending questions that were asked by the hostess of the show. Her parents (she was obviously adopted—they were Caucasian) were with her, stiff and nervous but beaming with sugary pride. She never once looked to them for help. She just stared right through the camera with a sort of mechanical vacancy to her face. Apparently, this little girl had caused a stir in the human-interest news community by being able to spell just about any word anyone could throw at her. To make the whole thing as trite as possible, the audience was allowed to do the throwing. She spelled Mississippi. She spelled astronaut. She spelled personnel. Not a particularly literate audience, but you get the picture. After each correct spelling the platinum-blonde-bimbo-journalist-hostess looked the word up in a weighty, leather bound dictionary and said breathlessly, "That's right," and the audience gave a collective "Ooooh."

"Hey dummy!" said Peter. "What did you get for number four?"

I snapped out of my trance. "Uh, 3.785×10^6 kilograms."

"What? That's not even the right units! Are you crazy?"

"Yeah. That's not even the right units. Are you crazy?" Useless snorted in agreement.

Having gone approximately three minutes without touting his intellect, Peter changed the subject. "Hey, I got a ninety-two on that Thermodynamics test."

"Quick, get the phone! I want to call home and tell everyone you got a ninety-two," Lenny snapped, interrupting a complex air solo.

"Yeah. Get the phone --" Before Useless could finish, Peter had him in a headlock and administered a barrage of noogies.

"So what did you get, smart guy?" Peter asked Lenny.

"An eighty-seven."

"Hah! I got an eighty-eight," Useless said emerging from a post-noogie haze. "What'd you get, Alex?"

The above exchange may not be entirely accurate because I had zeroed in on the TV again. The little girl spelled tribulation. She never reacted to the crowd or the lights or the adults around her. She was totally emotionless, to the point of being hollow. She spelled interrogative. It was as if she was wholly and forever resigned to her existence as envisioned by the people around her. She spelled oleander. She was defined by their expectations. The universe was merely rote, a thing to be memorized.

Now, don't get me wrong, I don't mean to suggest she was oppressed or abused. And I don't mean to suggest I actually knew what she was really feeling. Like me, she probably wasn't even unhappy. I'm sure she was just overwhelmed with being on TV and that in real life she was just an average seven-year-old girl, playing with dollies and pretty bows and whatnot. She was obviously very intelligent and the word skills she was learning would serve her very well in the future (I say this as someone totally dependent on a spelling checker). She would probably be very successful, go on to a good college, and maybe even move in with a trio of dweebs. But there was something in that visual that struck me, a vision of helplessness. Completely acquiescent helplessness. Why not scream in terror and hide behind mommy? Why not ham it up à la Shirley Temple? Either reaction—any reaction—would have been an affirmation of self worth. But she just stood there...

"Alex!"

"What? What?" I snapped-to again.

"What'd you get on the Thermo test?"

"I got right around the mean." My standard answer. I had no idea if it was true.

"What's your problem, man?" Lenny asked. "Are you pinin' for your Korean homeland?" he added, looking at the girl on TV.

"I'm not Korean, stooge. I'm American. I was born in Grosse Pointe."

"OK. Don't get touchy."

"Yeah ya stooge. He's American," Useless parroted with a major snort.

"Hey! You blew a snot on me!" Peter accused.

"Shut up, Peter. I did not!" Useless retorted cleverly.

This witty banter was interrupted by the phone. I took it upon myself to get it since I suspected the others would soon be involved in another round of noogies.

"Hello?"

"I hereby issue you a challenge, for the world championship of Midnight Frisbee Golf. Tee time in fifteen minutes." It was K.J., my real friend.

"I've got this test coming and I really have to study."

"A test? A test? Where are your priorities? You've got some kind of screwed up values system, buddy. This is of monumental importance. Daa-Daa-Da-Da-Da-Da-Da..."

I grinned, picturing him marching around his apartment to the Olympic theme. I suppose I shouldn't have allowed myself to be manipulated like that. I probably could have resisted the temptation but I turned back and saw that the dweebs had begun to belch the alphabet in unison. Some sort of bonding ritual.

"Fifteen minutes," I said and hung up.

I filed the little girl away, put on my jacket and was outta there.

APPLE PIE

TWO

Even today, when I'm dashing to a Midnight Frisbee Golf rendezvous, I run as fast as I can for as long as I can. The entrance to the Arb is less than a half-mile away so I can usually make it all the way at top speed. I try to stay conscious of my pace, taking long, leaping strides, visualizing each as a beat of my wings, progressively increasing their length to keep me at a constant pace as my legs weary. It is the beginning of a minor, fleeting, but accessible emancipation that will last until the next morning's alarm.

The Arb—officially Nichols Arboretum—is a vast University owned park, heavily wooded for the most part but with a few large clearings. Used as a combination ecological research center and student playground, it is criss-crossed with trails and footpaths. Some thoughtful soul attached sequentially numbered shiny red reflectors to trees and thereby created Frisbee Golf heaven. The Midnight part was our idea. There are no lights so, on a moonless night, simply navigating without cracking your skull on a low hanging branch is a challenge. Making par in the night is well nigh impossible. Plus, the place is closed at 10 P.M., so there's always the danger of a roving rent-a-cop to put the kibosh on the proceedings.

Never fear, K.J. and I were old hands at this. We knew the trails well enough to follow in the dark. We didn't always aim for the right tree, but as long as we agreed ahead of time on which tree we thought it was, there would be no problem. If we didn't agree, one of us would make up a rule on the spot to cover the situation. Whoever made one up first got his way. We also learned how to move silently and conceal ourselves when we detected the presence of others. When K.J. was going through his Bruce Lee phase he suggested we wear Ninja outfits so as to frighten off anyone who we happened to come across. I pointed out that as a red-haired ninja he would just look silly.

"Ninja's cover everything except the eyes. It enhances the karmic enigma of their being," he argued.

"No matter what you do," I replied, "you will never look Oriental." It's true. K.J. is a fresh-faced Irish-looking chap. He's reasonably attractive, but a miserable failure with women.

When I said he was my real friend I didn't mean it in the sense that he was loyal and true whereas others are not. I meant that he's part of the real world—a normal sort of person, a non-propeller head. We met at the restaurant where I worked part-time waiting tables. Almost immediately, we got used to each other in a very nonchalant way and started hanging out. Our friendship was utterly casual. Anytime we discussed solemn issues it was only to make fun of them, thereby confirming that the small concerns of our lives were vastly more important than anything that may actually have significance. In that sense, it was also the deepest and most indispensable friendship I had. For three years, he was my one link to existence outside the dweeb-cum-good-Asian-boy-persona I had adopted. Of course, I never discussed this with K.J., it being a significant topic. Sentimental things must be left unspoken between adult male friends, but still they are understood. And understood to be understood. Besides, he was usually too busy with some female crisis to care about any maudlin confessions of mine.

Back to the night in question.

I spotted K.J. in the isolated clearing where we traditionally begin. He had his official X-Files UFO Frisbee with little flashing lights around the outside and he was trying to toss it in the air and catch it spinning on his index finger behind his back. He hadn't heard me coming so he was toast.

I leapt out from behind a bush right next to him and let out a screech that they could hear in East Lansing. He stumbled over himself in shock and landed flat on his butt. It was a truly righteous hoot to see and I reacted accordingly. He responded by whipping the Frisbee at my chest.

"Jesus H.! I almost pissed my pants!"

"Oh, come on now. You haven't done that since you were, what, seventeen?"

"Psycho," he declared.

"How dare you force me to come out here and play when you know I should be studying?"

"Foolish Earthling. Your will is not your own. I control the vertical. I control the horizontal. Give me your wallet." He rose and dusted himself off. "Besides, you must be ready for your test. All the studying with your W friends."

"W?"

"Wimps, Weebles, Woosies."

"Actually, I'd call them Gs."

"Gs?"

"Geeks, Goons, Gomers."

"Oh, I see."

"Ws are more like social misfits. Gs are full-on freaks of nature."
"You're sure they're not Ds...Drips, Dweebs, Dorks."
"Yes, yes, you're right. There's a sense of hopelessness with Ds. I bow to your expertise in nerdology," I concluded.
"With friends like that you must be ready."
"Not even close. But that's the thing about tests; no matter how hard you bust your ass to do good, there's another one coming around."

Our game began, merely an extension of our conversation as always. "How's Sarah?" he asked.

"OK." That was a joke. Ha ha. My girlfriend Sarah's answer to virtually any question was "OK." K.J. maintained that made her the perfect woman. Not exactly true. I turned the tables on him. "Seeing anyone this week?"

"My last date turned out fairly well, actually. I talked her out of the restraining order."

And that's how the whole night went. We smart-assed for a couple of hours while getting devoured by mosquitoes and shredding our limbs on the branches. When we heard other people, we became silent statues until they passed, then picked up mid-sarcasm exactly where we had left off. When I finally got to bed I stayed awake for as long as I could, energized by the knowledge that once I fell asleep, I would have no choice but to eventually wake up and return to my life.

Is that the curse of ease and leisure, or is it just me? I hear about people hitting the lottery and retiring from menial jobs only to return after a few months because they're going stir crazy. They can't live without some outside force, some conflict, to stimulate them to activity and industry. Are their dreams and desires so mundane and unimaginative as to bore them without the constant interruption of work? I can't think of anything more pleasant than not having work or school, to sleep in after lying awake the previous night with my thoughts, to have a light breakfast with the newspaper or the mail and make too much of what I read. No drive, no ambition, no stress. (See what I mean about not being Korean?) But how do you get to be frivolous when frivolity is the only thing you enjoy? That is the real curse of ease and leisure. The only life worth pursuing is the easy one. But the act of leisure prevents the pursuit—you'll run out of money real quick—and the pursuit prevents the leisure—if all you want is leisure, work seems counterproductive. It is an eternal vexation; another question to send me swirling down the metaphysical toilet bowl. Or maybe I'm just lazy.

THREE

A great source of tawdry stereotypes about Asians is the hackneyed concept of arranged marriages. We are often presented with the quaint notion that such anachronisms still continue, which serves to generate a convenient old culture/new culture conflict, which inevitably leads to a shotgun marriage, more thoughtless ethnic mischaracterization, and lot of bad drama. I don't know if arranged marriages still occur in the cliche sense of two deeply traditional families contracting the marriage of their children at a very young age (as an American, it's hard for me to imagine such a thing). I suspect they don't, but if there was ever a couple whose marriage was so universally accepted as inevitable that it could be considered to be arranged, it was Sarah and me. A year ago you might as well have told a fellow that you knew an honest lawyer as told him Sarah and I weren't going to make it to the altar.

Sarah's family emigrated from Korea about two weeks before my eleventh birthday. Sarah wasn't her name then, it was Shin-ja, but arrangements were made and paperwork done to facilitate the proper Westernization, and she became Sarah. My eleventh birthday party was a quiet, genial affair. Most of the Korean community turned out as this was also where the Parks, Sarah's family, made their debut into our established Korean expatriate network. There were small gifts for me and treats for all the good quiet children, while the adults discussed business and gossiped. It must have been quite a relief for the Parks—especially Sarah, who was only ten—newly arrived in a strange land, filled with the anxiety of the refugee, to find themselves surrounded by friendly, sympathetic faces. In those days the Korean community was a ready-made support group. Now, of course, everyone is upper middle class comfortable.

Over the next few months it was my sworn duty to look after Sarah at school. Understandably, her parents had fears of her being mistreated. It was something of a nuisance as it distracted me from baseball and my friends for a while, but in retrospect I'm glad I wasn't selfish enough to resist. It was the least I could do, and never let it be said I didn't do the least I could do. I say it took months, though it's probably more accurate to lose the plural. Though humble and quiet, Sarah is very intelligent and personable with other females. Her English quickly went from good to better than mine, and she fell in with a crowd of very smart and snobby little girls that I hated. Her parents' fears were unfounded. Nobody could

APPLE PIE

mistreat Sarah—such a sweet, well behaved little girl—and not spend the rest of his life performing noble acts in penance.

Still, Sarah and I saw each other at school every day and we were both at all the Labor day picnics, weddings, funerals, birthdays, etc., that transpired in our ethnic circle. I don't know at what point our eventual involvement and marriage became assumed—like the majority of communication in my life, it was never spoken of directly—but it did, and you just don't cross expectations and assumptions in the Korean world without engendering feelings of betrayal. Unexpected behavior is the real enemy. Evil acts would have a chance for acceptance as long as they had the proper set-up, but something out of the blue, no matter how innocent or legitimate, is a strict violation of the holy safeguard of humble reliability.

I suppose the thing with Sarah and me was that everything seemed just right. Harmonious. She was a couple of months younger than me and, due to America being my land of birth, she would never achieve quite the level of assimilation I had. That meant the requisite manly dominance was pre-established. Not that it would have been a problem if we were equal in age and assimilation—Sarah was an appropriately meek Asian girl. When our fathers began to have business dealings together that made it a mortal lock.

As you've probably gathered, I lost Sarah over the course of the last year, and I sometimes feel a twinge of regret. But if you'd asked me at the time I probably would have expressed relief. It may have been about sex. Everything's about sex, isn't it? Sarah never expressed any interest in sex. Not a whit. And the only thing worse than being involved with a woman who fights your every move is being around one who completely ignores it. Hello! I'm puttin' the moves on you here! Could you please at least acknowledge my existence?

Knowing Sarah, I figured on unbridled reticence from the get-go and I thought I could deal with it. I didn't expect a complete absence of recognition. At least she could have treated me like a hovering mosquito and brushed me away, but I got nothing, not even a cold shoulder. You see, as a freshman, away from home for the first time, I was actually having sex from time to time. It must have been at a point where I was terribly satiated that I decided to formally ask Sarah to be my girlfriend. I knew sex was going to be sorely absent, but I fooled myself into believing that I was an adult and should begin thinking about my future. This was the future everyone expected for me and for us, so better be a man and get on with it.

Such is the effect of regular sex: it lulls you into a sense of triviality and your mind progresses to other illusions. I asked Sarah to be my steady and she said, "OK." Two years later I was cursing myself regularly.

Our dates, if you could call them that, were nothing more than a series of vignettes with a similar theme. The location varied—at home watching TV, at the movies, or just on a walk—but the sequence of events was as predictable as a tape loop. I'd move close—she wouldn't react. I'd put my arm around her—she wouldn't react. I'd softly touch her hair—she wouldn't react. Eyes forward, blank expression. How many times I longed for her to go limp in my arms, eyes flashing, breathing heavy, lips moist, and...

Anyway, going through this routine for about the five millionth time I suddenly had an epiphany. Sarah was the little girl who could spell. The little girl didn't run or cry, Sarah didn't slap me silly for being fresh. The little girl didn't laugh and ham it up, Sarah didn't shiver in anticipation and yield to sensual pleasure, clutching, writhing...

Anyway, on what turned out to be our last date, she greeted me at the door instantly, as if she was waiting with her hand on the knob. I was pleasantly surprised to find her roommates were not home—two big scary Korean girls. They were very protective of her and constantly placed me under the evil eye despite my unassailably respectful behavior. Subsequent events proved them good judges of character, but they had no way of knowing it back then. Sarah was all ready to go, dressed in a very nice single color sweater and a pleated, Catholic school-girl looking knee-length skirt. She wore no make-up, but her face was quite pretty in a cleanly sort of way. We didn't kiss. She just grabbed her purse and we left. She knew we would be alone in her apartment. Why couldn't she have met me in wearing a wispy half slip, or better yet, cellophane? Why couldn't she have given me a deep languid kiss when I arrived and led me to her bedroom where we could press our bodies tightly together, letting our burning desires build to the point of...

Anyway, the point is that it was over, whatever *it* was. I planned to tell her on that very night, but I needed a drink first so I suggested we walk over to the Del Rio bar. Once there, Sarah let loose and ordered a wine spritzer. I now recall that she was ordering actual alcoholic beverages with a bit more frequency, but it didn't register as significant at the time. That was one of the many signs from her that I misjudged, my hindsight being twenty-twenty. Also around that time, I remember seeing a copy of

APPLE PIE

Cosmopolitan mixed in among her schoolbooks. I thought she must have signed up for some goofy feminist theory class because she would never look at something like that unless she had to. Even that night at the bar there were other clues, like the fact that she initiated the conversation.

"Our fathers are starting that new business together."

"Hmm," I acknowledged.

"I think they want us both to work there after graduation."

"Hmm," (My version of "OK.") I continued, "Is that what you want?"

"It's OK." Of course it was. "Is that what you want?"

"It's what every good Korean boy wants."

She smiled, just slightly. Another clue. She understood my cynical comment and appreciated it, but again I missed it. I was so certain I knew what she was that I interpreted any evidence to the contrary as exceptions to the rule when, in fact, the rule was wrong.

"I don't know what I want," I said. She kept her barely perceptible little smile.

I wonder if she understood how true that statement was. No, I don't wonder, I know she did. Everybody did back then except yours truly. But I had other things on my mind, like dumping her. I did and still do respect her and I never wanted to hurt her in any way. I at least owed her the truth and, though painful, in the long run it would have been better to get it over with quickly. That would have been the honorable and courageous thing to do.

So I didn't say a word about it. I just stopped calling her.

FOUR

OK, now the whole truth.
 I had developed a devastating crush on this waitress at work. Actually, crush doesn't begin to describe it. She was beautiful and perfect. An angel. A goddess. Naomi—a lean, willowy blonde with all the trimmings. Our paths had crossed briefly a few times, and I quickly identified her as a flat-out killer, but I really didn't get all droolly over her until we worked a late-night, closing shift together.
 After nine P.M. or so, the dinner crowd would start to thin out enough that only a couple of waiters are needed to cover the whole floor. With all that space to operate in, Naomi, graceful as a gazelle in tight quarters, promenaded about like a divine, immaculate gull, soaring on the ethereal substance of the universe. That is, the universe as bounded my senses—and my genitals. The sight of her lithe, auspicious figure dancing through the room hit me like bus from a Jackie Chan film. Her sensuality gave the landscape a soft, steamy blur. She swirled and caromed among the tables, taking my libido along for the ride. Her recitation of the daily specials rang with all the heat and floral passion of a Shakespearean sonnet. The hang of her loose fitting khakis and the motion of her legs inside them could have sent the entire erotic film industry into bankruptcy. On her tiptoes, reaching to a high shelf, her shirt would pull slightly out of her pants revealing a sliver of the most heavenly flesh imaginable. Maybe it was just the contrast to the dreary anti-eros of Sarah, but I was way beyond any plateau of desire I had previously known. Spiritual and sexual ecstasy were converging to an apex before me, and I yearned to grasp and envelop it.
 But I had tables to wait on. And I had a duty to Sarah. And I wouldn't know what to say. And I was only an engineering geek with dweeby roommates. And she probably thought I was just another awkward Asian.
 Having transformed myself into a metaphorical eunuch, I started screwing up in deadly earnest. Whenever she was around, my ego would register eye contact, compelling me to devote a portion of my limited allotment of rationality to keeping myself in the real world. I freely admit to being a bad waiter, but her presence pushed me over the line into total incompetence. At one point I placed a dry martini in front of an eight-year-old, but only after delivering Moo Shoo Pork to a table of Hasidic Jews.
 This theme continued for a handful of shifts that we worked together. Then, one deathly fateful night, she spoke to me.

APPLE PIE

It was in the middle of dinner rush, an event that, due to my perpetual ineptitude, always causes me dire stress. K.J. is good at it. To him each new table is an opportunity to express some sort of wryly, absurd observation. Back in the kitchen, he generally keeps up steady patter of lighthearted facetiousness that ingratiates him to everyone. My first few times at dinner rush, I actually broke into a nervous sweat. My first two weeks worth of tips went toward replacing pit-stained white waiter shirts. I got over that, but never completely exorcised my uneasiness, probably because I have such a pronounced ability to mangle anything at anytime. But that night, in one of the all-time great historical examples of a blunder turning into a major victory, I picked up one of Naomi's orders by mistake. I was out on the floor before I realized it, so rather than return it to the kitchen I just delivered it to her table and made a mad dash back to get my own order delivered. Later, K.J. and I were jawing.

"Tonight. Same time. Same place. K.J. vs. Alex. Uno mas," he said, referring to MFG.

"I shouldn't."

"You should. There is nothing more important than our ongoing ultimate battle for truth, justice and the American Way."

"I should see Sarah," I moped.

"Such enthusiasm."

"I'm getting really close to breaking up with her."

"Are you crazy? Break up with a woman who says OK to everything. You're betraying the entirety of your sex."

"You know better."

"So break up with her. What's the problem?"

"It's like taking a puppy to be put to sleep."

"Do this: Make your move. None of this namby-pamby sneaking your arm around her or holding hands. Put your tongue down her throat. Feel her up. Either she'll give in to your savage desires like you know she's wanted to or she'll be so disgusted she'll kick you in the pistachios and throw you out. Either way, problem solved."

"I'm beginning to understand why you have such success with women."

Naomi reached between us for something, her shoulder lightly grazing mine. My heart stopped. She absent-mindedly brushed her hair back behind her exquisite, pink and perfect ear and I had to turn away. When she moved off, K.J. started rambling on about his latest romantic misadventure, but I didn't hear him. I was putting every ounce of energy I had into not becoming a blubbering mass of protoplasm. No sooner did I begin to gather myself than she returned and reached in between us again. This time she looked right at me and spoke.

"That was very nice of you to deliver that order for me."

"Well, I like to help out when I can," I think I said, although it may have actually come out, "Ahh foo uh wha gaaa." I consoled myself that I didn't actually slobber.

She moved on again, leaving K.J. looking at me with a blue ribbon grin of mockery.

"Just don't say a word," I warned.

The atmosphere changed when Bruce, the prissy little whiffenpoof of a manager, approached.

"Isn't it great how people come in off the streets and pay money just so we can have lengthy conversations in the back?" he sneered, his ribbon thin mustache quivering.

K.J. would have none of it. "Do I detect sarcasm, Bruce?" he retorted, looking at Bruce's nametag "...if that is your real name."

"Too bad you can't detect that there are tables that need to be cleared."

"Well, I came back here to chase a mouse and...Oh, there it is, on your upper lip."

K.J. stalked off in an overly dramatic huff. He could get away with that. I was chuckling at his little routine, but Bruce glared at me over his pointy little vole-like nose.

"As for you, I don't suppose you would condescend to wait on that table," he sniffed, gesturing to a rather sour-looking middle-aged couple.

"Uh-oh. Have they been waiting long?"

"They were teenagers when they arrived."

What a dick.

When I looked out at the table again Naomi was already taking their order. She looked up at me and winked. At least I think it was a wink. Maybe.

APPLE PIE

FIVE

There were mystical forces at work, I was sure of it. In my rearview mirror it's easy to identify the patterns and causality and seeming inevitability of my path to the present, but rarely do you see such things in real time. Even back then though, I knew something was up, if only vaguely. For the next few days I saw Naomi everywhere, and not just in the obsessive hallucinogenic sense. I actually saw her everywhere. The eerie karma of it confirmed my cryptically mystical sensations.

Three times I had to hide when I saw her. The first was in Steve's Lunch, a little greasy spoon-type diner where they serve some of the very best Korean food in Ann Arbor. (I should point out here that I never ate Korean food until I left home.) I happened to glance up from the counter and spotted her ordering carry-out. Panic stricken, I froze—Be-Bim-Bop hanging from my lips. Luckily I was able to regain motor control long enough to nonchalantly ease myself out of the scene and into the men's room. It was a close call; had she seen me there she may have thought I was Korean. After a good ten minutes, I got up enough courage to glance out of the restroom. She was gone. So was my food, the proprietor assuming I had disappeared. It was a small price to pay.

The next time was in Border's bookstore in the music section. At this point, I think it's appropriate for me to make a confession. I like country music. There, I said it. I'm finally out of the closet. You see, in a tragically hip town like Ann Arbor, that's just not acceptable. I'll wager long odds that you would never walk into Cafe Zola or Cava Java or any respectable coffeehouse and hear Randy Travis. Bravely, I would rather suffer the scorn and ridicule of my peers than live a lie. It's what I am and I can't deny it anymore. But I would have died of embarrassment if Naomi saw me in the country music section. Again, I beat a hasty retreat before I was spotted.

The third and last time I had to hide was just after I had taken a test in thermodynamics, the class that loomed so large as a symbol of my continuing state of frustration. The test itself was a surreal disaster. Every time I looked up, I saw everyone else scribbling away furiously while the best I could work up was partial answers to the questions in the hopes of getting enough credit to pass. I was unsure of all my responses, which caused me to stop and try to intuit out each answer, which, in turn, caused my mind to drift to all sorts of nonsense like food or sports or Naomi. At one point I recall trying to evaluate the underlying thermodynamic principal of one of the questions by drawing an analogy to the length of time to shake a martini to achieve the required heat transfer such that the gin would be appropriately cold but not watered down, which led me to think of James Bond, who liked his martinis stirred, not shaken, or was it the other way around, which was a whole other kettle of fish, which triggered this Casino Royale sort of fantasy I have, which made me wonder if Naomi would like to visit Monaco and would she be attracted to me in a tux or would it be too formal, and so forth. I also remember speculating that the professor was not actually homo-sapiens, but a super-intelligent pair of coke-bottle-lensed glasses who was making use of a human body as means of transport. As if in revenge, the body rose and said, "Time's up."

Afterward, I was surrounded by the Dweebs for the traditional post-test ritual.

"So how'd ya do? Whaddja get for number five?" Peter started.

"Which one was that?" Lenny encouraged him.

"Whaddja get! Whaddja get! Oh, I took the time to memorize all the questions. As if." Useless said making a feeble effort at mockery. A noogie assault was promptly initiated.

"Silence, Pig-dog. Whaddja get for number five?" Peter reinitialized the ritual but I was too flustered to let it continue unimpeded.

"What's the difference what anyone got? It's over. You can't change anything."

"Oooooooh, deep," they responded in unison sarcasm.

I always found this practice irritating, but I was particularly upset this time because I had probably not gotten a single answer right. I was just about to point out what a stupid and fatuous pack of doofuses they were when I saw Naomi out of the corner of my eye, headed directly for us. In stark panic, turned up my collar, turtled my head as deeply into my shirt as possible, and situated myself behind Peter's considerable girth. She passed on without noticing me.

When I saw her next—it was only a couple hours later—I knew it was *fate accompli*, if *fate accompli* means what I think it does.

I had escaped the Dweebs and was looking forward to a delicious lunch at Amer's Delicatessen. Narrowing my selection from the variety of stuffed pasta salads with the exacting eye of an art appraiser, I spotted K.J. at a far table. He was with some girl who I didn't recognize and he was waving me over. I jostled through to his table.

"My dude. Sit." He indicated an empty chair.

I noticed a hesitant timber to his voice and his subsequent look made it clear he was glad I was there.

"Alex, this is Brenda. Brenda, Alex."

Brenda offered a nod of acknowledgement followed by a plate of biscottis.

"No thanks," I said.

She gave the impression of being pleased at my refusal, as if to say, "Good, more for me." I turned my art appraiser eye on her. She seemed normal enough, if one were to judge the book by its cover, which works more often than the cliche would have you believe. Pleasant looking, if not spectacular; no abnormally pierced body parts, no twitches or immediately observable tendencies toward mental illness, no visible handcuff scars or other obvious remnants of a criminal life. Definitely a step in the right direction for K.J. I took at shot at conversation.

"So Brenda, what are you majoring in?"

She started to speak but thought better of it and reached quickly for a glass of water to aid her in swallowing her semi-chewed mouthful of biscotti.

"Ummm. Psychology," she finally answered.

"That's good."

K.J. and I exchanged glances as I began to see the light.

"So how did your test go?" K.J. asked, trying to pretend she wasn't really there.

"It was a surreal nightmare."

"Oh. Been there..."

I glanced at the plate and noticed the biscottis were all gone. My first instinct was to look for the thief, then K.J. said knowingly, "...may still be there."

Brenda was in the process of morphing into a gargoyle of a rather distasteful shade of purple. She was making the sort of whooping sound one would expect to make just prior to an alien busting out of one's stomach. By the time I realized she was choking, one of the busboys had serendipitously appeared and administered the Heimlich maneuver. She gave a feline furball hack and spewed a mushed piece of biscotti onto the floor. For a fleeting moment she seemed to be debating whether to pick it up and finish it off.

"That was close," she said, catching her breath. " I'm gonna get some more of these. You want anything?"

K.J. and I shook her off. She shrugged and went to the counter for another biscotti platter. It was amazing that anyone could eat so much so fast. On the other hand, she was apparently not burdened by the need to chew.

"What a display. Where did you find her?" I asked.

"She seemed all right when I met her. Of course, there wasn't anything edible within reach. Let's get outta here."

"You can't leave."

"Why not?"

"That amounts to ditching. You can't ditch, not after puberty."

"Who says I'm out of puberty? Ask anyone I've dated."

"Nope, not allowed." I was enjoying this.

"Who says?" He was getting nervous.

"Regulations."

"What regulations?"

"It's in the University of Michigan Code of Conduct. Ditching is only allowed when life or limb are at stake."

"Well, earlier today she said she thought I was yummy."

She was next in line at the cashier so, I had to let him off the hook.

"Whoa. Well, OK. Let's scram."

We scrammed, power walking until we were well out of devouring range.

"Whew. That was undoubtedly the worst date ever," K.J. declared.

"Except for all the others," I added.

Then I saw Naomi. She was across the street gliding effortlessly—floating, dancing, leaving a sparkling trail behind her.

"There's Naomi," K.J. said and we stopped and acknowledged her presence with a moment of silent honor. She drifted into a boutique.

"Uh-huh." I'm pretty sure my tongue wasn't actually hanging out. I don't think I ever reached that point, except metaphorically.

In the absence of the need to hide, the full effect of these close encounters unveiled itself. My inability to get her out of my head could have been passed off as a mere crush, but this business of spotting her everywhere I went drove home the aspect of divine providence that surrounded the matter. I knew what course of action lay before me. I was peacefully resigned to my fate. I would have to call her. I would have to ask her out. I would have to tell K.J.

"I'm going to ask her out."

K.J. laughed, the insensitive cad.

"I'm serious."

"Right. What makes you think she'd go out with you?"

"We were doing the eye contact thing at work."

"You can go blind doing that."

"You know what I mean. I think we connected...sort of...silently...maybe...you know."

"Oh well then, it's a sure thing." He shook his head. "Take it from me, death and destruction await thee."

"Nope. I'm gonna do it."

"At least she's not the type to Hoover the biscotti."

APPLE PIE

SIX

I spent the better part of the next morning alternately goosing up my courage to make the call and driving myself to distraction to escape my fears. After countless attempts to rationalize my inaction, I finally forced myself to go to the phone. Only I couldn't find it. It lay somewhere under the piles of laundry, magazines and dishes—all of it dirty—that covered every square inch of surface area in our apartment. I absolutely had to find it before my resolve faded. I began a furious search, knowing that at any moment this could become my excuse to abandon the enterprise altogether. Periodically, I blurted out "Where's the goddamn phone?" with steadily increasing volume, punctuated with grunts of urgent frustration. As I whirled about, flaying my arms like Woody Allen on amphetamines, my disposition was turning fouler by the minute. The fact that Useless and Lenny had chosen that time to play Battle of the Infantile Mechanoid Wombats—or whatever their latest obsession was called—on the Playstation didn't help matters. They had the volume turned up good and loud because they needed to hear it over the TV and the stereo. To top off the cacophony, they would hoot and screech regularly when somebody got killed, which must have been every few seconds.

Finally, I got an answer from someone.

"It could be anywhere," said Peter, taking his life into his hands. "But it's probably right here."

He lifted a pile of clothes to reveal the phone. Quick as a cat, I lunged for it, knowing full well that he was about to grab it and pretend to make a call just to get my goat. Lucky for him I got it first, 'cause he would have got one vicious, homicidal goat.

I pulled the phone over to a chair in the far corner of the room and made an aborted attempt at dialing. This was no time for ad-libbing. I had to have things scripted out in my head first (a sure sign of waning resolve), otherwise I was sure to mangle the proceedings.

"Turn that thing down, woudja?" I asked.

Hi Naomi, this is Alex Kim, you know, from work. You remember me, I delivered to one of your tables the other day. Yeah, the Korean guy. No good.

"Lenny, woudja turn that down please? This is important."

Look, I figured, she'll know who you are. You've worked with her plenty of times. Be informal. *Hi, this is Alex. How's it goin'?* Right. Then what?

"Woudja please turn that thing down?"

A pretext. Ask her if she wants to work a shift for you and then keep the conversation going. That was it. I dialed. Two rings.

"Hi, this is Naomi. I'm not home right now..."

Abort. "GODAMNIT! TURN THAT THING DOWN!"

"Bite me, douche-bag," Lenny replied.

"Yeah, bite me douche-bag," came the inevitable.

"Look, I'm trying to make an important phone call. Would you please turn it down just for a minute?"

"I am sorry, but I do not answer to douche-bags," Lenny answered in a telephone operator voice, sending Useless into the fetal position from laughing so hard.

As for me, all hope and resolve was lost. My courage had withered away, its disappearance coincidental with my opportunity to make scapegoats of the Dweebs.

"What a pack of dweebs!" There, I said it.

Peter leapt into the fray. "Well, that was a douche-bag kind of thing to say."

I threw the phone to the floor in disgust.

"And that was an extremely douche-bag thing to do," he continued.

I had to get out of there before Armageddon.

"Why did I ever get involved with you clowns!?"

Peter was up to the response. "Because you're a douche-bag. Everybody knows you're a douche-bag. Your every action is testimony to your douche-bag capacity. Your ancestors were among the most prominent douche-bags in history. The spawn of your loins will inevitably be douche-bags. That's why everyone is calling you douche-bag. Douche-bag. Douche-bag. Douche-bag."

Useless had turned beet red, certainly nearing hematoma, unable to get any oxygen from involuntarily whooping like a hyena. I bolted, but not without a quick detour to throw the circuit breaker, finally effecting blissful silence. The shock of not having at least three sources of background noise broke Useless' laughing fit. As I was walking down the hallway I heard him call, "Hey, ya stupid douche-bag!"

"I need to crash here tonight." I didn't pause for permission, I just burst past K.J. and pulled a beer out of his fridge.

"Mi rathole es su rathole. What's the problem? Locked out? Quarantine?"

"Excessive dweeb activity."

"Oh."

K.J. tossed a pillow and blanket on the couch for me. Surprisingly, the couch didn't disintegrate on impact. Clearly, the binding force of dried food and beer stains was stronger than it appeared.

"You want me to sleep on that?"

"It's not so bad."

"I don't know. There may be sentient life forms in there. Wouldn't that violate the prime directive?"

"If you lie very still they won't bite."

"Wake me up when you leave in the morning," I called as he left for the bedroom.

I gingerly eased myself onto the couch and allowed my thoughts to drift...

Naomi was so supple and willing as we lay bare on a bed of pure white linens, our bodies glistening from exertion. From beneath, she tickle-caressed my back with her long slender fingers and fixed her eyes on mine, guiding my movements with the subtlest of reactions. Such heat, such passion, such exultation. The only thing that spoiled it was that the bed was in my Thermodynamics classroom. I looked over and saw my classmates at their desks, scribbling away, but my seat was empty. Intermittently, they glanced sideways at me—at us—and snickered to themselves. Naomi reacquired my attention with her eager kisses and breathless nuzzling, but I couldn't keep going. I looked back at the class. By now, they were laughing out loud and pointing (Useless was setting the standard for this reaction). Coke-bottle lenses gazed at me from the front of the room and the human transport mechanism behind them just shook its head in dyspeptic judgement.

"GET UP!" K.J. shouted. "Jesus! I thought you were dead. As you requested," he slapped my head, "I'm on my way out."

I did not wholly regain consciousness. I only made a sort of moaning noise in acknowledgment.

"Lock up before you leave."

APPLE PIE

K.J. left. The next time I opened my eyes was two hours later, when I had exactly minus seven minutes to make it to class on time.

I am, by nature, a clumsy oaf. Under duress, it is my habit to stumble over most of the solid objects I encounter and generally knock things about, not infrequently injuring myself in the process. That morning was no exception. I tripped over and bruised myself on virtually every piece of furniture that K.J. owned until I was fully dressed and out the door, sprinting across campus at full throttle in the pouring rain.

It's a remarkable experience, falling in the mud. In the instant before one hits, one is lucid enough to know what's about to happen and accept that gravity will not be denied. One tends to slip into a serene state, not unlike, I assume, the reaction of a drowning man when he finally stops struggling and accepts the inevitable. By one I mean me, of course. An optimist would have been grateful that it happened after the start of classes so as not be witnessed by the student body at large, but I hadn't time to dwell on it in the circumstances.

The thing is, when I finally reached my classroom, about twenty minutes late by then, I couldn't go in. Not that the door was locked or that I was afraid to disturb the class with my entrance. I just could not make myself go in. No matter how much effort I put into taking a step forward I only wavered on my feet without actually moving my legs. I stood in the hallway outside the door—frozen, dazed, mud-soaked. The indistinguishable voices from within had that accustomed tone and timber of an engineering class. The professor's monotone and the occasional sincere question from a student in a higher pitch were familiar. Nothing unexpected or frightening was going on. It should have been a small matter to ease into a chair in the back without being noticed—not that being noticed really mattered.

So what the hell was my problem? My mind raced. It occurred to me not a single facet of my life coincided with my desires. Everything I valued was a dream. I wanted passionate madness with Naomi, but I was bound to Sarah. I wanted adventure and excitement, I would have settled for some fun, but I was surrounded by dweebs. I wanted to take risks and engender admiration and awe in all around me, but I was going through the motions of being an engineer, a good Korean boy. It was me. I was the little girl who could spell. I hated it; hated my life, and everything about it. I hated myself for not breaking free, but I didn't see that at the time. At the time, covered in mud, standing in that deserted hallway outside the classroom, I just knew I couldn't take it anymore. So I ran away, propelled by nervous breakdown-style fear worse than any dinner rush imaginable, back across campus to my apartment, pausing only to fall in the mud again.

When I reached my apartment I fought off the frenzy long enough to clean up, careful not to cast more than a fleeting glance at the mirror and be forced to confront my reflection. But the impulse to flee remained. My legs were quivering with nervous energy. Plus, I had to get out quickly because the Dweebs would return soon with stunned questions about why I wasn't in class, and I couldn't cope with that. I burst outside again like an escaped convict. I thought about staying with K.J. for a while, but that would have been too easy. As an act of self-affirmation it seemed to lack substance. So in my quest for a spiritual sedative, I performed what was and shall ever be one of the most pronounced acts of futility in my life. I got on a bus and went home.

APPLE PIE

SEVEN

Grosse Pointe is nice. It's wealthy for sure, and reasonably safe. Scorned by the fashionably urbane as shallow and hypocritical, it's actually a terrific place to grow up, with lots of upper middle class suburban side street neighborhoods filled with pretty solid citizens. Perhaps it was some lingering childhood impression of comfort and security that drove me home, I mean, aside from the bus.

From the bus stop I jogged through the labyrinth of Maple Streets and Walnut Aves, remembering my bike routes from childhood. I spotted my house at about a hundred yards; split level, two car garage, circle driveway, immaculate lawn and perfect hedgework. An outsider might point out that description fit just about every house in a three-mile radius, but not in my eyes. The position and context of my house in the block, city, country, and universe were irascibly imprinted.

Despite the fact that General Motors shamelessly clones cars and then affixes badges from different divisions on them, my father is a devoted Oldsmobile man. Sure enough, from about fifty yards away, I watched the latest model full-sized Olds sedan come oozing around the corner and pull into the circle driveway. All four doors swung open in unison with the trunk lid. I stopped to drink in the scene as the Old Man and a couple of his neighborhood cronies I recognized as Mr. Luger (pronounced Booger) and Mr. Brinkley (pronounced Stinkley) exited, along with my brother George. I had to admit a certain fugitive admiration for George, even though, as my immediately older sibling, he devoted a good deal of energy in his younger days to making my life unbearable. He had no discernible ambition other than to be hassled as little as possible and work even less. That was a mortal sin in my family. On the surface it might appear as though we're similar in our lack of motivation—George and me—however, my occasional laconic behavior is borne of indecision. George was active and intent in his pursuit of not doing anything. Whereas I had always looked at leisure and productivity as mutually exclusive, George understood the yin and yang of the game. The secret wisdom that both must exist allows him to work at minimizing productivity instead of eliminating it. He was the absolute master of doing just enough for just long enough to stay in everyone's good graces and convince the public at large that he was a worthwhile and productive citizen. Then he would cruise for as long as he could until people began to catch on that he's a slacker. Sensing this, he would just kick it into high gear again long enough to make them reconsider, then back to cruise control. It was a remarkable thing to watch once you saw it for what it was. I admired his skill and mastery of the game.

George lifted all the golf bags out of the trunk. There was a good deal of backslapping and forced laughter before Booger and Stinkley hefted their bags and headed off. George took his own and the Old Man's bag and carried them into the garage. Clearly, he was in butt-kissing mode, and I knew why. The Old Man had just started this consulting business on the side. George wanted to be the designated heir for it, undoubtedly because he had visions of hiring lackeys to do all the work with him riding the gravy train, but his timing was bad. He was at the point where people were beginning to get suspicious of his work ethic, and before he could snake his way back into approval, the Old Man struck a deal to bring Sarah's father in as a partner, which made Sarah and me the anointed heirs. None of this was ever spoken, of course. Just like it was never spoken that Sarah and I would marry. It was just known by all to be that way.

The Old Man went around to the back yard, running his hand along the hedgerows to verify their level and angle. I ducked into the garage where George was putting away the golf clubs.

I greeted him warmly, "Ho, pinhead."

"Twerp-face. Howsit hanging? What brings you back to the promised land?"

"A whim. Just getting' stir crazy."

"Too bad you didn't get here a couple of hours ago. You could've taken my place with the polyester posse."

"I wouldn't want to deprive you."

"There was one entertaining moment. At one point I thought Stinkley and Booger were going to come to blows over whose leaf-blower has more horsepower."

"Stinkley has the edge in reach, but Booger's got the sheer tonnage," I replied. "Why do you go on these things?"

"Duty I suppose. And politics," George sneered. At least he was honest about it. "You know how Dad likes to show off his oh-so-well-adjusted-apple-pie-American children."

"Lucky I wasn't there, then. When he introduced me at that new country club he said, 'This is my youngest, Alex. He's doing OK, but he needs to work harder.' "

"So? He tells me if I don't get married he's going to have to give that new company to you and Sarah. Have to. Dad always liked you best."

"Nuh-uh!"

"Uh-huh!"

"No way."

"Way."

This was our way of easing the tension. He was more bitter than I thought about that company thing. He knew the score just like I did but he was harboring the illusion that he still had hope—or maybe he really did have some kind of angle. Nah, the only thing that would help him would be for me to do something stupid, like break up with Sarah...

For all our snippy jostling, George and I always had a bond to ally us. Although he wasn't born in America, he was so young during the great exodus that he had no memories of the old country. Neither of us speak Korean nor have even the slightest accent. We never had to struggle to adapt to a strange culture. We have no appreciation of the old traditions, or so we're told.

"I'm thinking of dropping Thermodynamics," I said.

That caught his attention. "Really? Let me know before you tell Dad. I want to get my radiation suit back from the cleaners."

"And I'm thinking of breaking up with Sarah."

"Oh, sweet life. I'll be prancing my butt out of the doghouse real soon now. Darren and Penny will be here for dinner--"

"The children who lived."

"-- you can vaporize yourself in front of the whole family. This'll be great."

Mom was in the kitchen, of course. I adore my mother. She is an absolute saint. Just think of all the years she had to put up with the Old Man and his tyrannies—now that was a real arranged marriage. She was wearing a red and white checked apron, her hair was up in a bun and her brow was furrowed over some recipe. June Cleaver, Harriet Nelson and Carol Brady working in concert couldn't carry my mom's jockstrap, so to speak. I said, "Hi, Mom," and she turned and glowed at the sight of me, like...well, like a mom.

"Oh, honey! This is such a nice surprise! What are you doing here?"

"I just needed a break. And I wanted to see my mom."

I kissed her cheek and she beamed and giggled.

"Is that Alex I hear?" The Old Man called from the foyer.

"You take those filthy golf shoes off before you come into my kitchen!"

"OK, OK," the Old Man said with a condescending chuckle. "Alex, how are you doing in Thermodynamics this year?"

I realize that a "Good to see you" or a "How nice to have you visit" was too much to ask for, but I thought it might take him more than twenty seconds to broach the subject.

"OK, I guess."

The Old Man strolled in with his steady, short-legged Korean amble and gave me one of his arched eyebrow looks.

"You guess? You still need to work harder, eh?"

He kept strolling right on past me and settled into his armchair with the Wall Street Journal.

"Maybe you're spending too much time with Sarah. Is she distracting you?"

"Now stop that," Mom interceded. "Sarah is a good girl. She'd be mindful of that."

"Now, now, Mother. I remember what it was like to be young," the Old Man said, emitting another of those patented chuckles.

George parked himself in the kitchen to get a bird's eye view of this psycho's drama; smiling and shaking his head, reveling in his good luck. What in God's name possessed me to go home?

"Will you be staying for dinner? Darren and Penny will be by soon," Mom said.

"Sorry, I don't think so. I have to be getting back."

George, still grinning, looked at me and mouthed "chicken." I flipped him off on the sly. Did I really think I was going to be able to talk to someone there? Did I really think I could confide in one of those people and garner understanding and sympathy? Well, stupid me. I could have set them straight right away. I could have opened up and let my frustrations pour out. But they were so secure in their notion of me as what I was, I couldn't bring myself to challenge them. And that's what it was about—*them*. What would it do to *them* to find out I wasn't what they thought I was; that *their* world was a lie as far as I was concerned. Where did *they* go wrong would be the gist of the reaction. How could I be so heartless toward *them*. I did feel guilty at the thought of even possibly disappointing Mom, but what about *me*? I wanted to stay for dinner—I was hungry—but I couldn't stomach that schtick for another minute, and I couldn't make myself do anything about it. Futility incarnate.

I sought refuge upstairs in my old room until I could catch the next bus out. It would be confusing to them, me taking the hour-long bus ride there then turning around and immediately going back. It should have given them a clue that something was amiss with my psyche, but since it didn't violate any specific happy American family protocols, they would let it pass.

My room remained unchanged from nearly four years before, still reflecting my interests from various phases of childhood, heavily skewed toward the high-school epoch.

I guess my memories of high school are pretty good. I went to a private school of course. My class picture, still tacked up to the wall, contained fifty-three others, of which forty-seven were Caucasians. There have been a few—very few—brief, fleeting moments in my life when I allowed myself to be warmed by the sheltering convenience of being a racial outsider. I admit there is a certain appeal to finding a quick and easy definition of oneself in being a minority that I am not immune to. But, for me, the rational light of actuality has almost always revealed similarity rather than contrast. Only once in my entire life do I remember being the victim of an overt racial slur.

When I was eight, my best friend Timmy Maxwell and I were playing on the monkey bars when this big kid named Luke Coty confronted us. He was maybe three grades ahead of us and had a reputation for being a bully, as much as one can be a bully at a private school in Grosse Pointe.

"Hey, Kim," he said to me, then pulled the outer edges of his eyes back. "Ah so! Ah so!" He walked away laughing.

My best friend Timmy was laughing too, just for a moment. Then we went back to playing on the monkey bars.

If I were more aware (to use an Ann Arbor-ism) I might have used that incident to define myself as the Korean outsider who would never quite fit in, but would succeed in spite of the deck being stacked against him. The problem was I didn't feel all that hurt by it. He might as well have stuck his tongue out at me or called me a dork-wad, or something. It seemed to me

APPLE PIE

to be just another insult of the kind kids of that age constantly trade. What did make me uncomfortable was the next day when Timmy came to me with tears in his eyes to apologize for laughing at Luke's little inanity. He had obviously told his parents about the incident and had been hit hard with an anti-racism guilt lecture. My considered response was to shrug my shoulders and we went off to toss around a baseball.

Timmy was a good friend. His family moved away after a couple of years and I missed him for a while. Last I heard he ended up in the army.

I ran into Luke Coty a few years after when he was pitching for the other side in a little league game. He must have lopped a few years off his age to get in to a league I was in. I don't think he even recognized me. I wanted to slam a home run off him really bad, but I only ended up lining out to third after fouling off a few pitches. He eventually graduated and moved south where he became the youngest congressman in the history of the state of Arkansas and is now in the third of a five-year sentence.

Other than that, the only experience I have with prejudice is people assuming I'm Korean. Annoying, but not exactly the stuff of life-defining oppression.

The ride back makes a quick transition from vernal Grosse Pointe to bombed-out Detroit to officially renovated Detroit, followed by a good long stretch of I-94 where the only scenery is exit signs and an occasional glimpse at a small working class neighborhood. It stays pretty much the same from the Detroit border until you reach the Ann Arbor exit. I took the opportunity to sit quietly, eyes closed, and settle my mind. If nothing else, at least I wasn't as frantic as I had been that morning, but I was still hopelessly lost.

Glad to be back in Ann Arbor after my visit to another planet, I trudged back to my place where the Dweebs were engaged in their various trivial pursuits as if nothing had happened.

EIGHT

Professor Eyeglasses had summoned me. Dread. Even if I were not in the middle of my self-induced emotional turmoil, dread would have taken the day. That dour, dyspeptic wiener had taught both my brothers who, as you can guess, had done quite well in his class. Now there was me. I despised him; his judgmental didacticisms, his feeble attempts at humor—engineering humor—at which the other students would dutifully snicker. I despised him because I wanted nothing to do with his class, or the life it represented, but I didn't have the guts to break away.

I knocked meekly on his office door and entered. He was in his inveterate position; hunched over his desk with face in calculator, working it feverishly with both hands. As he turned to acknowledge me I decided that my earlier theory, that it was the glasses that were actually the living being and the human body existed merely to facilitate travel, was wrong. It wasn't a human body at all but some gargantuan amphibian.

"Please sit down," he intoned gravely.

He handed me my test. D+. I don't know if you've ever got a D+ on a test, but if you have, you know you are overwhelmed with a sense of wasted effort. If you were going to do that badly why not sack the whole thing and take an F. Out of respectful deference to the student-teacher relationship I mustered an appropriate cringe.

"I feel I must inform you that you're walking a fine line between passing and failing." He allowed a dramatic pause to let the horror of my position set in. "May I suggest you try joining a study group?"

"No, you may not suggest anything. Don't you understand that I don't give a rat's ass what grade you give me, you constipated old snot-gobbler!"

OK, I didn't say that. Maybe I should've. Actually I said, "I'm already in a study group." I rationalized the Dweebs into a study group so as not to be completely lying.

"Then may I suggest tutoring. If I remember correctly, your brothers were most excellent students. Perhaps they could help you out."

"I'd rather chew glass." But it came out, "They're very busy these days."

"I must admit this is new to me. In my experience with Asian students I have rarely encountered motivational difficulty. They seem to adapt to the academic rigors of engineering quite readily."

APPLE PIE

"I'm not Asian; I'm American. I was born in Grosse Pointe." This I actually said. I should've cold-cocked him. To this day I regret not delivering an overhand right to the nose. But you're not supposed to hit a guy with glasses, and he was all glasses. I settled for stalking out in such a manner that he could clearly see my displeasure.

The hostility that I should've used to slug that four-eyed geezer was going into wadding the test into a little ball in my right hand. My teeth ground audibly. My brow furrowed like an accordion. Students loitering in the hallway sensed my smoldering fury and parted to make way for my passing. I vowed, possibly out loud, never to set foot in his classroom again, no matter the consequences. The withering realization that I had nothing—nothing!—came to me. The sum total of my being and soul had a net worth of zero at the most, and was more likely deep in the red. I was going nuts! What could I do? Where could I go? Not home. Not school. Not Dweebs. Not family. Everywhere I turned was frustration. Worse, I knew it was my own fault. Coward! Do something! Breathing in gulps, capillaries erupting like Vesuvius, nausea spreading from groin to gullet, I could sense another wave of panic coming on and God only knew where I would run this time.

Then I saw Naomi.

The interval between classes had just ended and she was delicately slipping between the throngs into one of the large lecture halls. How would she handle this? Did she have some spells or incantations passed on from Aphrodite herself to ease the anguish? Everything about her was so smooth; no sense of struggle or effort. If she wanted something she probably just went after it, not stopping to fret over the effects on others. If she didn't want something she just walked away. *They* had to deal with *her* as she was—and *they* were probably grateful. I could read that in her every movement. Suddenly, a brilliant epiphany illuminated my path. In that instant I felt a certainty of purpose that I had not felt in years, if ever. My rage and confusion dissipated like mist in the morning sun.

A girl was sitting quietly in a corner of the hallway, looking at a class schedule, minding her own business. I approached her genially and politely asked to borrow it for a moment. The class Naomi had just entered was Thematic Social Violence in Literature and Philosophy in the Modern Age (and I am not making that up). I jotted down the time and place particulars. Apparently, I was still under the spell of my punch-the-professor adrenaline because when I handed the schedule back to the girl she was cowering and guarding herself with a can of mace. I carefully set the schedule on the floor and eased myself out of her line of fire, then headed to registration, dropped Thermodynamics and added Thematic Social whatever it was.

In fiction, that action would be called the turning point; the event that cast the die for all things to come. I don't feel comfortable with the sort of strict determinism that implies. From my view, all these events flowed seamlessly from one to the next and only formed a pattern in their whole. On the other hand, it's hard to deny that if there was ever a chance for me to follow a different path it was greatly diminished by that act. Naturally, I laid the whole thing before K.J. and took my hits.

"Thematic who? So what's the point? You're going to have to pass Thermodynamics eventually and you'll probably just end up with lens-man again."

"Maybe not."

"What about your father?" he asked.

"He'll just have to deal with it."

"Yeah, after all, he's a tolerant, understanding fellow."

"I don't care. I feel like a huge weight has been lifted off my shoulders."

That was true. All the anxiety and hostility had disappeared through a single action. I had slept easy and had no trouble getting out of bed in the morning. My other classes became more bearable as I was carrying such a no-sweat attitude. You see, I had confirmed my independence. No class could cause me such grief ever again because I knew I had the power to walk away.

I showed him the books for Thematic-yada-yada. Hemingway, Sartre, Orwell—the kind of stuff you should know about.

"This is education, not training," I said.

"Uh-huh," he cynicised.

"I can learn about ideas with this, not just analysis."

"Uh-huh."

"I want to be more than a pair of eyeglasses. I want to think more openly. To understand great themes. To—"

"—To live, to roam, to be. You seem to have good instincts. If you work at it, you might even get a daytime talk show."

I owned up. "Besides, Naomi's in that class."

"Ah," K.J. shook his head knowingly. "So it begins. Abandon all hope ye who enter here. Slow painful death awaits you. On the other hand, if you nail her it might be worth it."

Now that's what I call perspective.

NINE

I had no discernible rationale, short of a vague impression of cosmic certainty, to think Naomi had the slightest interest on me. You simply cannot overstate the sheer abandon and recklessness of my actions. Repressed milquetoast student, thought by most to be a dedicated, unassuming Asian boy, interrupts his studies and forsakes his settled life to pursue a beautiful girl on a hunch.

Illusion. Chimera. What a madman!

No one would ever accuse me of being cunning or calculating (or heaven forbid, inscrutable), but I tackled this challenge like a great general preparing to outmaneuver the enemy. My first day in my new class, we'll call that Class One, would be exploratory. I would arrive early, linger in an obscure corner of the lecture hall and watch for her. After she arrived and took a seat I would position myself well toward the back, out of the line of view. She had entered alone the day I saw her, we'll call that Class Zero, but I needed to be sure it was not an exception. If she habitually sat with someone else that would introduce an extra variable into the equation. I was sure she didn't, in the same transcendental way I was sure she was interested in me, but reason held sway over faith when it came to the possibility of finding myself being introduced to her boyfriend as "Alex, a Korean guy I work with." If she was sitting with someone, I'd need a chance to observe the creature and, if male, determine if it was a boyfriend or a boy-friend, then re-evaluate. If not, Class Two would mark my initial approach. Prior to Class Two I would loiter about again, but as soon as she sat I would make an inconspicuous beeline for the seat next to her where I would be pleasantly surprised to see her and strike up a conversation.

Not a bad game plan all in all, but now on a roll, I was compelled to evaluate further contingencies. There were two potential snags. A) She did sit with someone—potentially a boyfriend—but he was absent for Class One, thereby depriving me of the required intelligence and causing me to act upon a false assumption. Possible, but remote. What were the odds that he would miss the one class that happened to be my first one? Besides, spending Class Two in watch would probably not significantly decrease the odds of said boyfriend's accursed existence, but would certainly increase the odds that I would succumb to cold feet.

The other prospective problem, B) She really did have no interest in me and the whole thing was a lost cause, was not, in my estimation, worth considering. Reason did suggest that there was a chance of this. But in the absence of other information, reason did not indicate that it was the more likely of possibilities. When reason can't provide us a clear answer faith holds sway over reason. The risks are only as great as the rewards. It is better to have loved and lost. So in addition to faith and mystical vision, I had a bevy of syrupy cliches going for me.

Class One started as planned. I arrived early and found a remote, shadowy corner in which to slouch unseen. She entered through the same door I had seen her go in for Class Zero and eased through the crowd to a seat about halfway up, three seats from the aisle. I took a seat in the last row closest to the door, a spot that seemed most likely to make me, if not invisible, at least inconsequential.

Naomi sat alone. An indistinct girl sat to her right; they exchanged no words. On the left she placed her bookbag. Good news, serving to confirm my transcendental vision and so forth. I studied her for clues and indications that might give me a way into conversation with her next time. She paid attention to the Prof., but not too intently, and took notes fluidly. Her reaction to his pretentious humor was not laughter, but a sly, slightly crooked smile that, for some reason, didn't quite suggest a smirk. The Prof. prattled on for the duration, invoking names like Schopenhauer and Duhrer, which I recognized from the syllabus, and making remarks like, "...a hierarchy leading back to Spinoza..." and "...as you know from your Nietzsche..." and "...a point that was obvious to all except Ayn Rand..." That last one must have been enormously witty, judging from the reaction. I made a mental note to read up on some of these names, then it was over.

Everyone started to pack up and leave. The Prof. slipped on his patch pocket sport coat and gathered his notes, all the while engaging a handful of students with after class questions. There was an easygoing buzz as the attendees swayed into conversation with their neighbors or shuffled out the door to their next class. They were appreciably different from the concrete types in engineering. Clearly, school was not their primary focus, although I was certain they were at least as studious as I. They seemed less directed, more casual and comfortable; noticeably prone to light revelry (nobody was asking "Whaddya get?"). They wore the same clothes as my peers but they didn't look awkward or gawky, just carefree. They didn't bear the stamp of "have to" that dominated my world. They were more the "want to" type. From the snippets of conversation I overheard, the topics of discussion were music or love or books or politics, not school. Suddenly, I felt out of place and self-conscious.

"Alex?"

My mind was frantically searching for words. I don't know how long the search continued but it did occur to me that I had better say something soon or risk being taken for catatonic. If I had been paying closer attention I would have realized that she spoke my name—remembered me—and I would have felt a resulting upswing in confidence, but in my precarious state that didn't occur to me. I was planning on having until the next class to script our extemporaneous encounter. Now I had to just say anything and hope it came out right.

"Oh, hi Naomi. I just added." Good! Cool and understated; no coughing or stuttering; easy smile.

"I thought you were an engineer."

How did she know that? I never mentioned it to her. She may have just assumed it, me being Asian (in itself another, erroneous, assumption). If that was the case I was going to have to straighten her out, gently, but not just yet. On the other hand, wasn't I making an assumption too? Maybe she'd asked around, or maybe she once saw me with some engineering book. I nearly winced at the thought of her spotting me stumbling across campus, Dweebs in tow. It must have been something like that; she was far too angelic to resort to a common stereotype.

My first instinct was to lie, but if she had evidence...

"I'm trying to break out of the mold a bit." Another great answer! Back to back home runs. I was clearly on a cosmic roll. "Am I that far behind?" Good follow-through.

"Just a lot of reading. I'll be glad to share my notes...or maybe we can get together to study."

Ah ha! The eye contact thing again. "That'd be great. How about this weekend?" I said, careful not to press the point too firmly.

"Sure."

"I'll give you a call."

As she left, I wallowed in every sublime step she took until she was out of sight. Afterward, I had to remind myself to breathe.

APPLE PIE

TEN

In the days leading up to that fateful weekend I scrupulously avoided the Dweebs. I rose early (Imagine that!), left quickly and returned late. I prudently arrived at our common classes just after they started so I had to sit at the back, then exited instantly upon their completion before I could be confronted.

One time, I unexpectedly crossed paths with Useless in the Student Union.

"Hey man," I said as indifferently as possible.

Clearly ill at ease, he asked me why I had missed Thermodynamics for about "the last million classes." Without an iota of concern I simply said, "I dropped," and sauntered away casually, as if it were no big thing. I didn't look back at his expression, but I'm sure he was confused and more than a little fearful. Folks like the Dweebs, who are completely maladaptive and know it, have a number of defenses against the unrelenting and unpredictable variety of daily life, one of which is to draw a tight circle of wagons and never ever change, building themselves an emotional safe house where they will feel no pressure to grow and adapt. Poor saps. Imagine the terror my behavior must have caused them, suddenly to find themselves in a not-so-safe house, with an Indian brave among the settlers (to painfully extend the metaphor). It was going to be touch and go with them for a while.

The preparation process for my upcoming date was exhausting. I spent a good deal of energy trying to familiarize myself with the reading for Thematic Social Violence in blah-blah-blah. I approached the project with enthusiasm but, quite frankly, the subject matter was rather heavy going. Clarity and readability did not seem to be high on the agenda of the various writers. The Hemmingway stuff was OK, I got through a couple of chapters there, but Gertrude Stein was virtually indecipherable, and each subsequent philosopher seemed to leapfrog the previous in the weight and density. There were lines like, "Negative dialectics continues in the face of the solid intrinsic ontology of dehumanization." Sentences like that blur the distinction between highly educated deep thinkers and schizophrenic street people.

The only important thing was that I learned enough key names and phrases to keep a discussion going with Naomi, at least for a while, until we reached a point where our little study session gained academic validity, then I would lead us into more personal topics. This wasn't a date in the familiar sense—we had a veneer of professionalism to maintain.

As a matter of fact, there was the unmistakable stink of scam surrounding the whole mess. They say you don't know what you are capable of until your back's against the wall. They're right about that. As I look back on those days I draw the comforting conclusion that when it's really important, I can connive and scheme with the best of them. I read summaries of the authors' works in reference books like *Masterpieces of World Literature* and *The History of Modern Philosophy* and *Cliffs Notes*. I even read the dust jackets of the books to gather the basic info required for my little kibitz. To further enhance my façade of thoughtfulness, I found some obsolete textbooks in the library and reworded the review questions from the ends of the chapters in a more contemporary and casual manner. I rehearsed how to answer questions in an open and non-committal way, "I see what Schopenhauer was getting at but don't you think..." or "Camus doesn't impress me; doesn't it seem that..." or "That begs the question, what would Hegel say about...", gearing each question to generic circumstances rather than concepts directly from the readings. After all, I'm an expert in generic circumstances.

The next topic of agonized preparation was my choice of clothing. I tried a couple of fairly radical (for me) get ups—doo rag, reversed baseball cap, extra long shorts, etc. Fortunately, I had no illusions of being hip so I could see that I just looked really, really stupid. Nice slacks and a button down shirt was an option, but this wasn't a date, remember? Finally I settled on the most casual attire I had that didn't cross the line into sloppiness: a pair of khakis and a loose, single color pullover.

Post study conversation was another matter. The key was to get her talking and follow her lead. It didn't matter where she took the conversation—anywhere was just fine with me—but it was important not to lead the conversation directly because I was the one playing a game, trying to step out of my usual life. Observe and adapt, would be the watchwords. I found out through discreet inquiries at work that she was originally from Arizona, and there would be clues in her apartment—books, CDs, posters, etc. I was tentatively confident ad-libbing on that front.

So I was ready; except for one last minute concern: Had I over-planned? Was I going to come off too perfect, too scripted? I needed something spontaneous to fall back on; an impromptu occurrence to hide any potential suspicions of recitation. I needed to arrange for something unplanned to happen. I needed to think really hard about whether rationality had deserted me entirely. I was thinking too much. And thinking too much about thinking too much. So after I had a final review of my kibitz notes, I laid out my clothes and watched a half-hour of a football game, consciously making too much of the outcome and the controversial plays to distract myself and assure a clear mind when the zero hour came.

On the way over to meet her I performed a visualization exercise. Athletes will often visualize a competition in its entirety prior to the event; they report that this makes them more at ease and confident since, in their minds, they're performing for the second time around. I visualized the perfect date with Naomi: about half an hour of philosophy discussion; out for a cup of coffee and some after-study conversation; gentle flirting and long lingering looks; then back to her place for pure animal sex.

The funny thing is, that's exactly what happened.

Well, pretty close anyway. After admitting me and begging I make myself at home she poured some wine and we moved smoothly from superficial preliminaries to the specific topics of the class. So far so good, but all my scheming and strategizing had taken a toll. I found myself in a state of mental exhaustion from trying to keep up on the academic discussion while staying keenly aware of any potential opportunities to get events shifted to a more personal level. The business end of the proceedings had run well past the ideal half-hour limit and I found myself suddenly overwhelmed by a desire to sleep (which is my standard reaction to wine). Luckily, after the opening minutes, I didn't have much involvement in the process since it had become less of a dialogue and more of a lecture. She spoke with sincere intellectual passion, totally absorbed with the topic. As she spoke she would work through the logic of the concepts, peppering her speech with "I get it," "Ah, that's it," and "Oh, I see." With some effort I was able to maintain the guise of interest (no one goes through three plus years of college without developing the ability to appear rapt with attention while actually cruising the astral plane), then I noticed her ankle. She wasn't wearing socks and I saw she had a tiny tattoo of a rose on her left ankle. Her slender, slight, flawless left ankle. This, combined with the still life of a vase of roses over the sofa and the rose potpourri on the coffee table, gave me the opening I needed. At an opportune pause in her soliloquy I grinned amiably and said as incidentally as possible, "I'm detecting a definite rose motif."

Mission accomplished.

"That's very observant of you," she responded with a sly smile. "I've actually had a thing for roses as far back as I can remember. I don't know why. It may have something to do with this movie I saw when I was little, *Mrs. Miniver,* it's one of my earliest memories, watching that movie with my parents, but I couldn't tell you anything about it now except that a rose played a significant part."

"When I was a kid we--" I started, but stopped when I realized she wasn't done yet.

"Or it could be a sign of sexual confidence, but I'm not a Freudian. Do you want to go out for coffee?"

"OK." That was a relief, in my depleted state I desperately needed the caffeine.

As she went to get her coat she called, "What about when you were a kid?"

I raised my voice. "There was this family back in Grosse Pointe and they used to raise--"

"Café Espresso Royale is right around the corner. Is that OK?"

"Sure."

"I'm sorry, you were talking about Grosse Pointe."

We set out for coffee.

"This family used to grow roses and enter them in contests." It had seemed like a relevant conversation extender when I first formulated it, but after two false starts I had instinctively truncated it into a single, terse sentence.

"I don't think it's right to compete over such beautiful things, it lessens them," she continued.

"I'm really not competitive at all," I offered. "In fact that's kind of a sore point with my father."

"Oh, I see. He's pushes you to succeed, doesn't he?"

"Yeah, in a big way."

"He's very dominant and patriarchal isn't he?"

"I suppose."

"Now I get it. That's why you're so conflicted. You want to be more artistic and open but he's pulling you back. I'm not being too personal am I?"

"No, not at all. You're right, he only thinks about achievement."

By now we were sitting on one of the big, comfy sofas sipping on cappuccino.

She nodded knowingly. "I think independence is the most important thing, in the stoic sense."

I nodded as knowingly as I could.

She continued, "I've always pretty much done whatever I wanted, you know? I don't mean I, like, was spoiled, I just pursued whatever interested me. I never needed to justify anything as productive and purposeful."

She went on for a while about her personal experiences with freedom of spirit and their connection to her interpretation of platonic beauty. I was concentrating on maintaining eye-contact and thinking lascivious thoughts as a way to subliminally suggest we should have sex. There was a noticeable slowing of the conversation, allowing the eye-contact to become long lingering gazes.

We ambled back to her place—my knees buckled slightly when she locked her arm in mine—and started nuzzling and kissing. Falling into bed with her was absolutely seamless, as routine as if I had been through a thousand visualizations, which I may have. But this natural, thoughtlessly casual act changed absolutely everything.

You would think that my seminal memory of such an event would be of sweet carnal bliss; the primal pleasure of intimacy with an angelic, nearly mythical figure. Not so. The first impression that comes to my mind is a sense of achievement, but not masculine sexual achievement. The achievement I speak of is the rational achievement of successfully imposing one's will on the random, unfeeling universe. Like Newton's Laws or a Bach fugue, that night stands in defiance of the probabilistic nature of existence; hard evidence that great things can be planned and executed, they do not only happen at the desultory whims of chaos.

As I lay in bed with Naomi pressed against me, my thoughts were a swirl. It started with self-doubt; maybe she slept with everybody. She had told me there was no one serious but what did that mean exactly? It advanced to performance anxiety; did she fake it? This can never be known. Apprehension about what to say in the morning followed. She was to settle that quickly in the A.M. by suggesting we get together again soon and we should talk about things after our next class, wisely giving us both time to get comfortable with the new state of nature. Yet even in the face of these nagging little discomforts I had an overriding feeling of control. Everything was going right; just as I had planned. I decided that must be what the world is like for most people; people who aren't so repressed and constricted that they don't dare risk disappointing anyone, even at the expense of their own happiness. Free People. Yes, everything had changed. I was now going to be one of the Free People, and I would find that everything would start to go right. All my worries melted in the warmth of this realization and the heat of Naomi's body. I had purpose and, more importantly, confidence. I finally nodded off and slept as deeply as I ever have.

ELEVEN

Sometimes I wish I were inscrutable. The next day I saw K.J. and he knew instantly what had happened from the look on my face. Conversely, I knew that he knew from the look on my face from the look on his face. We were wading our way through the flotsam of humanity that loiters around the University of Michigan, enduring assaults from pamphleteers, hucksters, dead-heads and faux preachers, each espousing some solemn cause and earnestly educating our troubled society with their flyers or solicitations for action. The correct response to these people is to accept whatever they offer with a kindhearted smile and be certain not to make more than fleeting eye contact. As a supplement, it's a prudent plan to make it obvious that you're involved in some thoughtful activity and don't want to be bothered, although that doesn't insulate you from the most zealous. For our activity, K.J. and I chose to try to ascertain what would be the definitive act of bravery for the new millennia.

"...OK...OK. Here's one: You stand outside *Ms.* magazine headquarters—scalping hockey tickets." That was one of mine.

"Hmmm. Pretty good. The element of danger...yes...yes...and futility. A fair test of courage indeed. But here's the ultimate. Are you ready for this?"

"I'm all a-twitter."

"You go to a Nation of Islam rally, walk up to Farrakhan and say, 'C'mon Louie, be a mensch.' "

"Oh my. Oh my. You win. You are the master."

We must have let our guard down since an odd woman confronted us with the sickly sweet smell of incense about her, dressed like a Satanist Annie Hall. She was wielding a pamphlet and an otherworldly gaze that didn't quite achieve serendipity. Her speech was obviously prepared, but not overly strained.

"Witches are not evil. We are a culture with an inherent compassion toward nature. We only seek a symbiotic and enlightened relationship with all living things. In that sense we are the true heirs to the Native American cultures of the past. In a witch, all energies are balanced; the physical, the intellectual, the spiritual, the ecological, and the sexual. Please attend our seminar on the Wiccan Way and raise your awareness."

APPLE PIE

A mediocre performance all in all, not over the edge like the chubby pseudo-preacher I happened across the week before who advocated salvation through Jagermeister. K.J. and I walked on unaffected.

"I slept with Naomi last night."

"Now that is courage. I think I had sex once. Does being stood up count as sex?"

"Sure. It's best to think of the glass as half full," I suggested optimistically.

"How about a drink in the face?"

"What kind of drink?"

"Wine."

"Possibly. An '87 Napa Cabernet, definitely. White Zinfandel, never. Your better Bordeaux count as threesomes."

"What about: 'If I ever see, hear, or smell you again I'm going to rip your balls off and stuff them down your throat'?"

"Depends on how she meant it."

"So is Sarah broken-hearted?"

"Oh she's fine. Of course she doesn't know yet."

"Ah," he said accusingly.

"I'm not looking forward to this. It'll really hurt her."

"What makes you think she won't just say 'OK'?"

"What if she starts crying? What do I do then? Jesus, I'm no good at hurting people's feelings. If the hangman pouted when I resisted the noose I'd probably say, 'Oh don't cry, it's OK, I'm glad to be hung.' How do you go about breaking up with a girl?"

"I generally get her alone in a quiet, neutral place and sit silently while she says, 'I don't think we should see each other anymore.' Works like a charm."

"Hmmm. Well I haven't talked to her in couple of weeks; maybe she's figured it out by now."

"Good strategy. I've found avoidance to be a highly underrated solution to many problems."

"Well said."

The Dweebs had become very ill at ease. As I had feared, the trauma they felt at my self-alienation was enormous. I continued to dodge the study sessions, avoid them in class and generally be as off-putting as decorum would allow, and they weren't dealing with it very well. When you're a dweeb, surrounding yourself with other dweebs is an emotional necessity. No matter how socially inept you are, as long as you have a few kindred souls in your immediate circle you have a shield against the outside world and the pain of adaptation. But when one of the gang realizes the pathos of the situation and makes the bold move to normalcy you are reminded that, in the light of verity beyond your sheltered walls, you're still a dweeb. That was the cold shower of reality that I thrust them into with my behavior. They occasionally made small overtures to bring me back in the fold, such as being almost quiet when I was around. At one point, Useless even asked if I wanted to play a game of Death Battle of the Mutant Robots on the Playstation. He'd even let me win.

I was not unmoved by all this—I suppose it goes back to my self-destructive desire not to disappoint. But I had come to realize that your friends can drag you down more efficiently than anything else except your family. All changes are a shock to friendship, and when your friends have an image of you that you need to get beyond, the discomfort you feel from their discovery that maybe they don't know you so well after all, the corresponding prospect of your friendship being suddenly invalid, and the sense of betrayal they feel from their dashed expectations, is a strong disincentive to making the change in question. For me, my continuing faith in the forces of harmonious fate tipped the scales, not that that made it any easier on the Dweebs.

We slipped into an uneasy routine wherein they continued pretty much as before, but with greater effort expended toward not offending me. I assumed the role of the tolerable outsider. I had silently resolved to move out at the end of the term and felt more or less settled about the whole situation.

Thus, I paused to thank God one day when I returned in the evening and they were gone. It must have been a sci-fi convention or some such provident thing. I went into my room to change and just as I had my pants half off the phone rang. You can probably guess by now that the delay caused by my subsequent collisions with stationary objects meant that the machine picked up before I did. And a good thing too; it was Sarah.

"Hello. Hello. This call is for Alex Kim. Please call Sarah, if you would like to... We can go out, if you would like to... Good-bye."

Wow. I think I said that out loud, I was so surprised. It was totally out of character for her to call me. Once again, I was so confident in my conception of her and her limitations that I concluded that it was an anomalous occurrence brought on by my boorish behavior, not indicative of something subtle and unappreciated. All it did was get me feeling guilty for about thirty seconds until the phone rang again. I still didn't have my pants all the way on and so performed a slapstick instant replay. The machine picked up again and this time it was Naomi.

"Hi Alex. I thought you might like to..."
"Naomi. I'm here."
"Were you monitoring?"
"No, I just got in."
"You were, weren't you?"
"No really, I just got in."
"I'm going to a poetry reading tonight, then a party. Wanna come?"
"Sounds great."
"Cool. Pick me up about 7:30."
"I'll be there."
"Cool. See ya then."
"Bye."

TWELVE

Poetry reading. Snore. Still, I'd give it my best fake rapt attention expression and chalk it up to experience. The point was we were going to be together and that probably meant sex afterwards.

Things couldn't have gone more effortlessly when I picked her up, in contrast to my discomfort at the outset of our first date. We kissed gently at her door and exchanged comfortable small talk, full of little irreverences, as we walked to the reading. She hooked her arm in mine again and I shivered in exhilaration, hoping this would become a habit. She was gliding in that graceful languid manner that she had, floating through life and taking me along for the ride. When I was with her, every conflict and fear, however fundamental and inescapable, faded into the background scenery while the camera followed the main characters. The world cast a much less intimidating shadow. Sarah, Dweebs, family—all vaporized in her presence.

She asked how my reading was coming along and segued into an analysis of one of the philosopher characters from the syllabus, I can't remember which, and the essence of his relevance. I didn't hear a word of it. I just drifted easily away on the quality of her voice, soothing like gentle music. It wasn't what she said, but that *she* was saying it. When we reached The Shaman Drum Book Shop, where poetry was about to happen, some guy was playing Irish-folk guitar and singing like a wounded duck. She continued talking through the supposed music. It drowned her out completely but I never let on that I didn't hear her. I merely contented myself with watching her lips—the lips I had tasted—and standing in awe of their sculpted perfection.

I was shaken out of my rapture when the music abruptly stopped. The crowd quieted and cast their eyes to the microphone. A short fellow with an unkempt beard took the mike and began talking about how good it was to see everybody and what a wonderful night we had ahead of us and blah-blah-blah.

"Who's...," I started, although it took me a moment to determine the right verb for a poetry reading, "...performing?"

"Odium."

We worked our way to front of the small crowd where the most intent were sitting cross-legged on the floor.

"Odium?" I resumed.

APPLE PIE

"Yeah."

"No, really—Odium?"

"She's one of the most respected poets in the city."

On cue, a short, bone-skinny woman with a multi-hued crew cut stepped up to the microphone. She was dressed entirely in black, and had the contents of a small hardware store pierced into her skin in various nonstandard places. Throughout the performance she spoke in an expressionless, unwavering monotone and seemed only marginally aware of the corporeal universe, speaking into the microphone more out of habit than an understanding that that was what needed to be done to have people hear her. The patrons maintained a respectful silence.

amidst events both tepid and cold
a chiseled darkness aloft
tomb or cradle empty
cradle or tomb
embraced
and invisible in the sullen mist.

Hmmm. OK, that one would take some thought. Although, judging from the oohs and ahhs of the audience, the point was apparent.

"Wow. That was chilling," Naomi said. She seemed to get it. Odium continued:

a word or the word
rhymes with most others
simple goes the song not
without effort
higgledy-piggledy

Again the audience was way ahead of me. To a man they discerned humor. I chucked lightly so as not to look the fool.

Naomi leaned over. "She'll be at the party tonight."

I was a bit uneasy as we walked to the party. In this arty crowd I was bound to be a fish out of water, and there was no chance to mentally prepare for contingencies. But I was not a pessimistic fish. I looked on this as an opportunity to flail my way back into the bowl. On the way, we discussed non-academic, common ground subjects—movies she liked (I didn't bring up Schwarzenegger or Stallone), hassles at work, restaurants. She seemed to carry strong opinions on all topics, in contrast to my instinctive equivocation. There was some minor give-and-take to our conversation, just enough to give some vitality to our interaction, but no more. My balancing act in this regard was flawless. More importantly, her arm was still linked with mine. It was never like this with Sarah. Oh yeah, Sarah. In a flash, I was reminded of Sarah's phone call and began to feel guilty again. I almost begged off for a moment to find the nearest pay phone to call her and lie about everything being all right. But there was no phone in sight and the impetus was fleeting.

"Are you nervous?" Naomi asked.

"What? No. Why would I be nervous?"

"You put on a good act, but I can tell this isn't exactly your usual scene."

"It's fine. I'm enjoying myself."

She smiled and, I swear, she twinkled. She actually sparkled like a jewel in the night. I wasn't nervous. After that first night with her I was never nervous around her again. I was apprehensive—generically apprehensive, but that's pretty much my constant state.

APPLE PIE

THIRTEEN

The designated party house was west of the downtown area in what might be called the townie side of Ann Arbor. East of campus stand the massive dormitories, indistinguishable from office buildings, designed to shelter underclassmen with commercial efficiency. To the south stand the fraternities and sororities, mostly in modified private mansions of old; stately facades behind which people are drinking beer right from the tap. Immediately west of campus is downtown Ann Arbor with its trendy shops, bistros, and bookstores. Yet further west are rapidly aging, single family homes that have been altered to contain several tiny apartments. These are rented seasonally to students for astronomical prices despite that they are, without exception, in an advanced state of disrepair. This arrangement provides the illusion of long term residence; of a neighborhood, not merely temporary student habitation. It's here that the class of Ann Arborites who have fallen from, or have yet to achieve, the academic grace of graduation reside: the English major who discovered a formula for getting steady grant money; the environmentalist who stumbled on to a paid position with Greenpeace; the distracted drop-out who abandoned all ambition and took a low stress, low status job on the University payroll; the hedonist who, enamoured of the Ann Arbor night life, took a full-time job in one of the local retail shops and enrolls for one or two classes a year, in an effort to make the party last as long as possible. (Truth in advertising: I live on the west side now.)

    Muffled music led us to the correct door. Inside, the music was louder but no more distinct.

    We were greeted by a portly black man wearing what looked like a pink flannel bathrobe, although it was intended as something more stylish. It would have gone well with fuzzy pink slippers. He greeted Naomi with faux kisses on each cheek and made a few comments. The tone and inflection of his voice, along with a couple of laconic hand gestures, suggested that he might have been a homosexual. More specifically, a raging queen.

    "And who have we here?" he asked, scanning me vertically.

    "This is my friend Alex."

    Gently placing his limp hand in mine, he almost imperceptibly pursed his lips.

"Well, there's wine and beer and some divine stuffed mushrooms and, oh, you must congratulate Odium. She was named artist of the year by The Society for Poetry, Peace, and Gaia."

"We were just at her reading," Naomi mentioned, employing the correct verb.

"And Julian is back from the rainforest," he added.

We grinned and Naomi led me past him to get a beer. I could feel his eyes on my butt as we walked away. No, not literally.

"You aren't homophobic, are you?"

"Of course not," I said dismissively. Not exactly a question that can be answered in the affirmative in polite company. I did wonder for a moment what would have happened if I said yes.

We reached the food table where I took a beer, a fine microbrew, and a moment to assess the partygoers. They did seem to be a weird lot—no, correction: diverse lot—at least as far as appearances went. There was a penchant for black attire, as well as little round glasses. The effect put me in mind of beatniks from the fifties, which I found oddly appropriate. Hair was another matter; it ranged from shaved heads (on both sexes, assuming there were only two) to uncut and unkempt manes, and it came in a stunning array of hues. And then there were the piercings; the choice of location made me cringe in more than one instance. I was to learn later that this was the desired affect; a social statement about the convergence of pain and fashion. *Pret-a-porter* performance art.

"There's a lot of unusual people here," I said, instantly regretting it.

"Just non-conformists," Naomi corrected.

I made the acquaintance of a handful of people, including a couple of PhDs who were running a local Mexican restaurant; a fellow who sported a sort of reverse mohawk and whose stated profession was an Urban Lovecraftian Rap Troubadour; an older guy with an eyepatch, who went by the name of Doobie and made confused references to 'Nam; and lastly Odium herself.

I had just opened my second beer when I glanced to my left and she was standing next to me, close enough to be considered a personal body space invader. She stood motionless, with the eerie calm of a potted plant, implying she had been there a while, though I had sensed nothing. She almost directly looked at us with an off-center stare that was far too intense to ignore.

"Hi, Odium. Congratulations on your award. Do you think it will help your career?" Naomi asked.
Her gaze moved directly at us, then through us.
"Yes," she intoned.
"It looks like a book contract is the next big step."
I gave it a shot. "I'd like to hear some more of your poetry."
No response; not even a shift in the stare. Maybe she thought I was asking her to recite some on the spot, which believe me, I wasn't.
I tried to clarify. "If I knew when your next reading was..."
Still nothing.
Naomi whispered, "You have to ask a direct question. She doesn't respond to statements or commands, only direct questions."
"What, do I look like Alex Trebek?"
Naomi gave me her wry smile and went off to get us a couple more drinks. In possession of the key to Odium, I gave it another shot.
"Have you been a poet long?"
"All my life. Do you and Naomi have sex?"
This chick was out there. I thought she might have been trying to draw an analogy between how long she had been a poet and whether Naomi and I had sex, and the connection went over my head. I was giving her too much credit. She was simply curious, and having no sense of reticence or tact, she just asked. Fortunately, before I had to answer, Naomi returned and suggested we go over to meet another friend of hers.
Julian was a skinny, flimsy sort of character that I took an instant dislike to. He was a victim of the rare and tragic strain of tetanus that caused the face to lock into a perpetual expression of indignance. He and Naomi exchanged cheek kisses, which didn't improve my opinion of him, and he immediately mentioned that he was "back from the rainforest."
"How are things in Brazil?" Naomi asked.
"It was a real eye-opener. A wake up call for the soul. I did it all; worked with the native tribes, went on research expeditions with zoologists, stood down bulldozers at construction sites. It was truly fulfilling to achieve that level of participation. I can't wait to go back again."
"That's terrific," I supposed.
"So are you going to return to local activism now that you're back?" Naomi continued.

"I don't know. Ann Arbor has come to seem very small and sheltered to me."

"It must give you a real sense of accomplishment," I offered. "I'd love to have an adventure like that some day." I was doing my best.

"You can. Go. Right now. Don't let anything stop you."

This was intended as sage advice from one who'd been there. For the most part, I'm willing to give people the benefit of the doubt when it comes to obnoxious behavior. I don't believe in knee-jerk cynicism, and I try to accept people as sincerely and non-judgmentally as possible. But this guy deserved to die.

Doobie—the eyepatch 'Nam guy—suddenly appeared. "Jungles. Man, just like 'Nam."

Doobie and I got into an extended conversation. It was like being in some sort of symbolist film. Like I said, Doobie tended to ramble about his experiences in 'Nam, often reciting phrases that had no common reference or discernible connection to each other. But he said them in such a thoughtful and conversational tone that you were left with the impression that if you gave it enough thought it would make sense.

"Losin' buddies, man. Know what I mean? It's like one minute you're sifting through the ashes for clues, and then you suddenly realize that you can buy 'em at the PX at a discount. You never forget that."

Still, it beat talking to Julian. The rest of the time I spent making small talk with the various denizens, cleverly keeping my conversations shallow and carefully avoiding controversial comments on their pet obsessions (they all seemed to have at least one). In turn, they were able to get just familiar enough with me to assure themselves that I was no threat, and to have no objection to my appearing at subsequent parties. I was so stiffly conscious of my role as an outsider applying for membership that I didn't even loosen up after a few drinks. Naomi however, was plenty loose by one-thirty, when she tossed me my jacket and led me out the door with the teasing comment, "I have something to show you."

As she led me by the hand I dragged her back from crossing each street without looking. The thing was, the light kept turning in our favor the instant we reached the curb. She giggled harder as each crossing-light fell into sync at the instant I began holding her back. By the time we reached our destination I was the one leading her and stopping her in the middle of each intersection to kiss and giggle some more. It was like we were giddy children; or at least the way I imagined giddy children would be.

We reached a tall parking structure, trudged up the dirty stairwell to the top, and sat on the edge. Dangling our feet over the side, a good eighty feet from the ground, we looked out over the city, all alight and milling with sound and movement.

"Whoa. They oughta build these things a little more steady," Naomi said, teetering a bit from the alcohol.

Sitting there in the crisp evening, looking out and down on all the activity, I was overwhelmed with optimism. Everything was actually going right. My natural tendency at such times is to look out for booby traps; readying myself for the unknown annoyances and disasters that lurk in the shrubbery. A good sense of yin-yang can really take the edge off the pain (along with cutting the pleasure off at the knees), but for the first time in my life I felt the hope of elation. My recent experiences were so exhilarating that they outweighed the sum of my life to date, with a good bit to spare.

"You see how it is," Naomi said, gesturing to the sky. "The city lights just go back and blend in with the stars. It's like there's no borders, everything is just the same thing, but only with a different aspect."

I saw.

APPLE PIE

FOURTEEN

The principal theme of an hour of so of free entertainment—poetry readings, coffeehouse guitarists, bad movies that no one will pay to see—followed by a party at somebody's apartment pretty much defined my social life for the next couple of months. On average, this would occur three times a week. The remainder of the evenings were spent in literature or philosophy discussion with Naomi, where she would explain to me what everything really meant. My other classes suffered, but only a bit, and let's face it, the regular sex made up for any educational detriment. Also, I began to get better acquainted with the most common fixtures at these parties. Julian was almost always there and I was almost always able to tolerate him, if for no other reason than Naomi seemed to admire him and I didn't want to cause her any discomfort. I was careful to keep a close eye on him though, suspicious of his motives toward her. He seemed to keep himself in line in that respect, but I noticed he always ate and drank at a casual but constant rate throughout the night. Devouring copious quantities of food and drink that other people have paid for was the quickest way back to the rainforest, I suppose.

The gay host from the first party turned up nearly every night, always around midnight. His name was Ronnie and he was involved in some sort of contentious homo-romantic relationship with an entity named Garland, who I never met or even saw. He told terribly funny stories about their misadventures, romantic and otherwise. Maybe it wasn't the stories that were funny but the dramatically flamboyant way he had of telling them. In any event, I came to look forward to seeing him. At least he wasn't talking about grave and important matters of the moment like everyone else. That was a pleasant relief.

And Doobie never missed an evening. He belonged to the school of thought that held that 'Nam was the seminal cosmic event from which all existence sprang. Not that he could have articulated it so well. He possessed no serial memory of events in 'Nam, instead making random associations to whatever was the topic of discussion. Talk about music, he'd be reminded of the cool songs on the Jukebox at Hi-Lo's roadhouse in Saigon. Talk about cars, it would occur to him that everything he knew about cars came from his work in the unit motor pool. Talk about rock climbing—hey, he lost a buddy like that over there.

APPLE PIE

What was more remarkable than his obsession with 'Nam of the past, was how he managed to find his way around in Ann Arbor of the present. Nobody knew how to reach him. To my knowledge he didn't have a phone, or even an address for that matter, but he always made it to the parties. At first I had pictured him wandering randomly from door to door throughout the city until he stumbled on the proper festivities. In reality, if reality applied to him, he never had to go to such extremes. He did his wandering during the day and invariably he would run into someone who knew the location of the night's festivities. I was doubly surprised to find out that this was the same way Naomi learned about the goings on. As I came to realize, Ann Arbor is really a small town core of people—real townies—who tend to travel the same pathways and live lives deeply embedded in the city, surrounded by a large majority of others for whom the city is just another suburb with some colorfully pretentious shops and restaurants, or a place to go for nine months out of the year and drink while your parents think you're studying. This informal network was a natural development in that respect; an ingenious control mechanism. Everyone who was anyone in this little subculture knew where to go to run into the others. With no formal lines of communication, undesirables could be passively excluded. Nobody could verifiably think himself intentionally left out or be offended by not being invited. There were no invitations in the proper sense. There was never the possibility of a "Why didn't you call and tell me about your party?" when no one was ever called—they all just heard it from so and so. Everyone maintained plausible deniability.

Another common theme was Hearts. As the parties wore down someone would break out a pack of cards and a few of us would play Hearts, often until dawn. These games brought out interesting, and very indicative, aspects of the personalities at hand. A typical exchange might have been scripted as follows.

RONNIE: I refuse to believe these cards. I'm sorry, I just cannot accept these cards. Oy.
ME: It's not a dream. This is real.
RONNIE: Well, pinch me. I mean, I can't believe these cards. Oh, it was very good of you to pass a low heart sweetie.
JULIAN: You have to pass a low heart. It's fascist not to.
ME: Sieg Heil.

JULIAN: I don't care. I'm not in it to win. I can just enjoy the game. The score doesn't matter.
ME: Then you don't mind taking the queen.
RONNIE: Oh, puh-lease. Don't get me started on Garland.
ME: Is Doobie dead or something? I mean, he hasn't moved in a good twenty minutes.
RONNIE: I told you, don't get me started on Garland.
JULIAN: I think he's OK. He looks peaceful.
RONNIE: Oy. Garland got like that once. And in Canada of all places, on our way back from Niagara Falls. The border guard picked us out for a search, which was totally raw of him, and we had this bong in the trunk. I mean, no pot, just the bong. I mean, this thing was left over from, like, high school prom night. Imagine that. Busted. A night in a foreign jail. And that's what Garland looked like. I swear he didn't move all night. Oh my gawd. He just shot the moon.
JULIAN: I warned you about passing a low heart. Now you all have to lose because of Alex's greed and shortsightedness.
ME: Bite me.

You'll notice Naomi didn't have a speaking part. She was like that during the games—completely out of character, silently intense—a closet competitor. But she usually won. This didn't bother Julian, who only played to educate the rest of players, and by extension, we as a society. Ronnie, at least, was genuine.

In any event, the five of us—Naomi, Julian, Ronnie, Doobie and me—became a circle of, not quite friends, but familiar and cautious acquaintances. Actually six of us. Odium was always there too, but rarely spoke, except when one of us, suddenly aware of her presence, asked her a direct question.

Around that same time I made a couple of decisions. 1) It was time to move out on the Dweebs. I know I had decided that before, but I often have to decide to do things several times before I actually do them. I had visions of hosting an edition of one of those parties I had been attending and, as it stood, I couldn't even mention where I lived for fear that someone would happen to drop in and get a glimpse of my life *au natural*. More importantly, 2) I would become a philosophy major.

At this point I'm going to suggest you pause for a moment to think about the impact of that on the time-space continuum. If you have cognized (if cognized is a word) long enough, you will have concluded that it could not be anything less than the End of All Things. Maybe it was fate—again. Maybe, if it wasn't this, it would have been something else to turn my life upside down. To say this decision changed my life is true, but to further state that if I hadn't made it things would be different is impossible to know.

I discussed both decisions with Naomi, of course. On the first, she was ho-hum and claimed to not care about who my roommates were; she wouldn't call me a dweeb no matter who I associated with. She did mention that she had lived in a variety of places around the city and would be glad to help me look for a new apartment.

She was more enthusiastic about the second decision. Encouraging to see me broadening my search for fulfillment was how she put it. Then we made love to emphasize the point.

Afterwards, I was basking in the glow, or actually glows, there being the physical glow of having made love to the most exquisite creature on earth, and the psychic glow of having a planted direction for the future based on the above decisions, as we were walking hand in hand across campus. It occurred to me I should get in touch with K.J. and set up an MFG session to bring him up to speed on things when I saw he was coming toward us.

"There's K.J.," I pointed out.

"You're friends with him, aren't you?"

That didn't sound good. She asked that as if she had just recalled a bad habit of mine and wanted to know if I was still indulging it, as if she might innocently ask Charles Manson, "So, are you still doing the mass murder thing?" If my interpretation was right, I needed to make it clear that I was not going to give up K.J. There would be no easy acquiescence from me on this topic.

"Best friends," I said with a certainty that I subsequently undercut by asking, "You don't like K.J.?"

"It's not that I dislike him..." she said, expecting me to drop it at that.

"But..." I remained in pursuit.

"Well, he's a little hard to take sometimes, you know, all that sarcasm. He comes off rather immature."

"Come on. How could anyone not like K.J.?"

Before she could answer, he was upon us.

"Nice shirt," he said to me. "Getting ready for a long, strange trip? You know, I have a lava lamp that would go well with that."

I was wearing a tie-dyed shirt that Naomi had bought for me. Nowadays I use it to clean my toilet (sorry, a bitter moment). But K.J.'s comments didn't help my position. This was confirmed by the snide, sideways smirk Naomi tossed at me.

K.J. continued, "So what are you two up to? You wanna do something tonight?"

"Well, we're going to the coffee house tonight--" I started.

"--with some people from philosophy class." Naomi quickly took possession of the response before I could invite him. In this she was right. Turning K.J. loose on the party crowd would have been awkward for me, and probably downright painful for the others. I don't expect he would have let their pretensions pass unassaulted. K.J. looked at the ground for a moment, or beat, as they say in Hollywood, and I knew he saw the situation for what it was.

"Thanks for asking, but I think I'll pass," he gracefully responded. The whole scene was too touchy for my taste. K.J. is a pretty tolerant and understanding guy, but friendships are the most fragile of things; I wanted very much to make sure no feelings were hurt and that this didn't have any deleterious effects.

"Believe me, you wouldn't enjoy it," I proffered.

"Yeah. A lot of deep talk and stuff," Naomi added; damn her.

I kept at it, "How about some MFG?"

"Just let me know when," he responded ambiguously enough to keep me in the dark about his feelings.

I wasn't about to let it go. "Listen, we'll double soon with you and..."

"...Toni," he said.

"Toni," I confirmed.

"Yeah, that sounds fun. I'd love to meet her," Naomi added, this time without sabotaging me.

"Let me know when." More ambiguity. I would have persevered but he brought things to a close. "Well, I guess I'll see ya at work."

Dammit. Now I had a mess to clean up. I couldn't be angry with Naomi. I'm not so naive as to believe that everyone I like will all like each other.

She could have been more tactful though, or at least been quiet. All I could think of to say was, "How could anyone not like K.J.?"

"I told you I don't dislike him. Do you really think he would fit in with us tonight? Do you think he'd enjoy the kind of evenings we have?"

She was right about that, but she missed the point. I should have taken the opportunity to explain a few things to her right then and there. Naturally, I just put patching things up with K.J. on my to do list and let it go.

I had a good five, ten minutes there without a single negative or troubling thought. No, it didn't last, but things were still on the upswing, generally speaking, and maybe I could repeat or even extend those minutes once I got things cleared up with K.J. And Sarah. And my family. And school.

FIFTEEN

I readily found new digs on my own. An apartment just down the street from dweeb central came available at $750/month. For that low, low price I got a ten by ten room, a kitchenette furnished with 1950s vintage appliances, and a tiny bathroom with a stand-up shower. To move up to one full bedroom would have cost an extra $115/month. To move down to a similar sized one-room job in the basement of a rat-infested dive would have saved me only $25/month. So, like the baby bear, my porridge was just right. It really didn't matter. It was mine and I was going to live my new, improved, everything-going-just-right life in it.

Peter was the first to speak. He didn't raise his head from his magazine, he just gave me a snide "felicitations" upon hearing the news. Lenny only shrugged. Useless was nearly venomous. "That's fine. We already have someone who wants to move in."

So be it. Because of my betrayal—my self-outing as a non-dweeb—they had chosen to make me the enemy. This, I suppose, was healthy. And true, in essence.

Things mellowed a bit as move-out week continued. A little each day, I moved my possessions to my new place. It must have seemed to them like I was dismantling their castle piecemeal.

At the end, Lenny told me not to be a stranger. Peter never said goodbye, just "See you in class." (I hadn't mentioned my planned transmigration to philosophy.) Useless never looked me in the eye. At my final exit he shuffled up to me with an "aw shucks" posture and extended a limp hand. I resisted the temptation to say, "I'll miss you most of all, Scarecrow." With all the sincerity I could muster I just said, "I'm gonna miss you guys."

I saw them in class over the final weeks of the term but we never spoke. Then they were gone. We spent three and a half years living in each other's pockets and within a few days I wondered if they had ever really existed.

Julian was not exactly the type to move heavy boxes as there were no clear socio-political implications to the activity. Doobie would have found it too confusing and retreated into 'Nam flashbacks. Ronnie—well, Ronnie was a queen and you just don't ask a queen to perform manual labor for the reward of a couple of beers; frankly, it's below them. Odium would have needed too much direction, all of it in the form of a question. Asking

Naomi would have violated all precepts of chivalry. So I asked K.J. to help me with the heavy stuff. It gave us a chance to talk, by which I mean it gave me a chance to make sure there were no bad vibes left over from our previous encounter.

"It's not what I would call spacious," was his comment regarding my apartment.

"I don't need much. I don't own anything."

"Then you can put it anywhere." He circled the place, checking it out. "Glorious view of the dumpster. You can take out the trash without leaving the safety of your home. And I see they've cleverly economized by putting the toilet in the shower stall. I guess you can hold your head high and say you pee in the shower."

"I always have."

To his everlasting credit, K.J. was tolerant of my and Naomi's—mostly Naomi's—tactlessness at our last meeting. He shrugged it off with a "No problem" and an "I understand," which I found rather scary. Scary, because I wasn't sure I would have been so magnanimous in the same circumstances. Could it be that K.J. put more effort into our friendship than I did? That thought really, really bothered me. I always thought of us on equal ground in terms of our silent embracing of each others ways. Our forced informality assured that serious sacrifice was never a necessity and as such, there could be no significant imbalance of obligation. I shuddered at the thought of me not being worthy of K.J. and what that would do to both of us. In the hopes that a personal revelation might work to restore any lost camaraderie, I broke the news about my intended change.

"Philosophy?"

"Philosophy," I stated.

"Philosophy?"

"Philosophy."

"Are you gonna cut the soles out of your shoes, go live on a mountain, and dispense wisdom?"

I found the sarcasm reassuring. "Philosophy."

He gave an evil chortle.

"What's so funny?" I asked.

"I was just picturing your father when you told him. That must have been pleasant."

"I'll let you know when it happens."

"Avoidance again. Stick with the tried and true methods."
Internally I grimaced, reminded of Sarah.
I explained the practicalities. "The Old Man would cut me off cold turkey. I can't deal with that right now, what with paying for this place and everything. I got to figure out a way to break the news without breaking myself."
"This is a borderline scam—no, this qualifies as a full-on scam. Not that I disapprove."
"I'll tell him. When the time is right."
"Breakfast would be a good time, since you'll be toast."

That day, as it turned out, was probably the highlight of my neo-bohemian period. Things were cool again with K.J., I had my very own place, the girl of my dreams, and even the twin terrors of facing Sarah and confronting the Old Man seemed too small to worry about. When the group went out that night, out of sheer exuberance, I did one of the silliest and most out of character things I have ever done. I read poetry on stage.

This venture into performance art had been fluttering about in my mind for a considerable amount of time; ever since Naomi proved to be so keen on the stuff. Getting poetry is something I will probably never do, but then, you don't have to get it, you can just write it. The low quality of my work would be passed off to inexperience, not incompetence. It was a win-win setup. I would either be esteemed for my clever poetry if it turned out to be good (not), or admired for my daring gumption, but either way my stock would rise, and I might even engender a little envy. Lord, I was getting to be a top-notch conniver, wasn't I?

Originally my plan was to hit the library and plagiarize some very obscure looking actual poems, but that was risky. If someone asked me directly if they were mine I would have had to lie, which I would have, but I'm a lousy liar. I'm even a worse liar than I am a waiter. Not only that, it would have been perfectly in character for one of those clowns to have a minor in obscure poetry.

Then I found a web site that actually created poetry on the fly —http://www.tenthousandmonkeys.com. One simply typed in a few words that were to be prominent in the piece and the software would cleverly complete a poem of random words in a choice of one or two different styles. A few attempts produced a couple of winners that precisely captured the disjunctive sentence fragments and portentously vague imagery that go over big with poetic types.

That solved the plagiarism issue, but it just wasn't me. I mean, who's to say I'm not a poet? I mean, all these people I was hanging with claimed some sort of artistic pretension, but I didn't see anything resembling art. I mean, if they could be artistic without actually doing art, so could I. So in a first class artistic snit, I sat down and wrote poetry; wrote from the heart, with relevance to my experiences (write what you know). In about ten minutes I had a developed a finely crafted little bugger, ready for recitation.

Thursday night was always open mike readings at a place called Marigold's Milieu, a new age music shop cum loom supply store cum coffee house in the basement of a juice bar cum used bookstore cum Native American art gallery called A Horst of a Different Color. Marigold was an overweight, nearsighted, 50-ish woman with unkempt gray hair, who wore garish floral print dresses, which I took to be an effort to recycle curtains from defunct motels, punctuated with symbolic silver jewelry—ankhs, crosses (but not Christian-type crosses), pentagrams, etc. I never met Horst.

Unbelievably, the place was full. We had all squeezed around a couple of small circular tables we had pushed together off toward the back. I looked around the room trying to determine which of the attendees were poets, and which were displaced engineering geeks. Marigold stepped up to the microphone.

"Welcome to open mike night at Marigold's, for the best in poetry and performance. A couple of announcements before we get started. Thursday there will be a round table brown bag luncheon and book signing with Agatha LeJune, author of *The Path of the Moon is Mine to Follow*, the painfully exhilarating story of the search for love and wellness of an adolescent Maori woman raised in a Tibetan nunnery. And next Tuesday at four-thirty will be the monthly meeting of the Stouthearted Sisterhood of Seasoned Vegans; all humans are welcome to attend. Without further ado, who'd like to be our first performer?"

My hand shot straight up. Even without looking at them I reveled in everyone's amazement. Ronnie might have said, "Oh my God." I think Julian actually choked on his espresso. He may have thought I was joking, but not for long. Per instructions, I took the stage, *sans* ado.

Tangled webs woven alone
Upon reflection chill to the bone
Merciless manipulation the tool
Ending in blight for the targeted fool
Escape impossible
Acceptance, resign
Invoices rendered for crossing the line
Selective apathy a true rebel's tool
Toward unfettered pastures, fickle young fool

    Silence was my biggest fear, for a moment I thought that that was my reward, but as soon as everyone realized I was finished I got a nice hand. A pessimist would have called it a smattering of polite applause; still, better than silence. They once booed Dylan offstage. I think it was Dylan, but I'm not sure if it was Thomas or Bob. Anyway, when I sat back down the reaction from the group was mixed.
    I took a deep breath. "Well, I did it."
    "It was nice. I liked it," Naomi said to be supportive. It may have been the only poem she ever heard that she didn't bother to analyze the deeper meaning of. Not good for me, but at least she admired the effort, as I had planned.
    "And it even rhymed," Julian said with snooty facetiousness.
    "It was precious. Absolutely precious. Wasn't it precious?" chimed in Ronnie.
    Let them proffer their dry vindictive sarcasms. Let them shrug in indifference. They couldn't come out and criticize me directly because they had never done it. They only had the pretense of it, not the act itself. They could never pigeonhole me or stereotype me again. How many uptight Korean students recite their own poetry? Exactly one. Me. Chew on that next time you settle on a cliche to define me.
    Suddenly there was a fit of laughing. It was Odium, the poet laureate of Ann Arbor. She had been at the end of the table staring at the floor. She laughed without averting her eyes from her stare.
    "I liked it," she said and returned to silence.
    There, a professional opinion. It's not many a poet that can claim that reaction from Odium without asking her directly.

APPLE PIE

I wore my attitude like a badge of honor for a good ten minutes (another good ten minutes, I was up to twenty total), then slipped into boredom as other, less talented poets took their turns. I don't specifically remember making love to Naomi that night, but I'm sure I did. I would have.

SIXTEEN

I was still glowing the next day. I had thoughtfully scheduled a spontaneous gesture of affection for Naomi, so I bought a single red rose from a street urchin and met her outside her morning classroom. I was decorously sheepish as I handed it to her and she was appropriately demure accepting and saying, "How sweet." We kissed and she went into her class as I watched in admiration for a brief moment.

Spinning clockwise on my heels to leave I found myself face to face with one of Sarah's roommates. I immediately spun counter-clockwise only to see the other roommate.

Let me take a moment to debunk another stereotype. Contrary to popular opinion, not all Asian women are petite and lady-like. To say the least, these two were bruisers. K.J. maintains that he once saw their names mentioned in the sports page as having won the Jackson State Prison boxing tournament. That may have been exaggerated, but their breadth and width could not be. Furthermore, I knew them to be very protective of Sarah, as I once was supposed to have been in grade school, but there was no way I could ever have been as terrifying as these two behemoths. They closed ranks as I backed away until I hit a wall. Trapped. They appraised me as a butcher might size up a healthy Holstein. A Clint Eastwood tightness came into their jaw lines. My thoughts were divided between my strategic objective of not hurting Sarah, which would require me to come up with a quick explanation, and the tactical necessity of escaping with my life when, from between them, previously hidden by their bulk, Sarah emerged, her eyes watery.

I started to say something, I don't know what it would have been other than an indecipherable stutter, but she ran off sobbing leaving me to face the juggernaut sisters. The one on the left made the first move. Thankfully, my reflexes didn't fail and I managed to cross my legs before she could take her preferred course of action. She adapted quickly however, and delivered an open right hand across the face. I count myself lucky that she hadn't closed her fist or I'd still be paying the dental bills. My good fortune dissipated, along with my breath, when number two hammered my solar plexus with a savage left hook. Having inflicted the desired amount of pain they ran off after Sarah, leaving me doubled over on the floor to the applause of passing students.

APPLE PIE

The distance I had achieved from my previous life had lulled me into a dreamy state of hope and idealism. Sarah was all but forgotten, except for occasional twinges of fretful foreboding that I had no trouble rationalizing away in short order. Now I was like a felon who had suddenly felt the firm, inevitable hand of the law grasp him from behind. This latest incident (Or would calamity be more proper? How about tragedy?) triggered an ongoing fearful anxiety—the lingering presence of reality—that I could never quite shake. That and a sore mid-section. I skipped classes the rest of that day and sulked around my apartment occasionally groaning from the combination of a double Korean amazon mugging and a guilty American conscience.

I had to talk this over with K.J. Wisely, I didn't attempt to talk it over with Naomi. Bad form at the least, I would call it, discussing former girlfriends with current. Plus, I was ashamed of myself for letting the situation fester until Sarah felt herself humiliated and I actually was. Plus, I didn't want analysis or wisdom, I just wanted someone to lighten my load. We had scheduled—K.J. and me—an MFG session after work that night, but owing to the fact that the wind chill was about minus infinity, we opted to pick up pizza and beer and head to my place to mange.

"So it's this real haughty-taughty type with his leather faced wife, you know." K.J. was retelling an incident that occurred that evening that was destined to become part of his growing food service legend. "And he says, 'You're expecting a tip aren't you, young man? Well I'll give you a tip: Never give money away when you don't have to,' and he starts laughing. So I say, 'Thank you very much sir, and allow me to return the favor: Don't goose the perky little waitress booty when your wife is in the rest room.' He better sleep in his iron jockstrap. Oh, look..." He picked up a piece of paper that had been slipped under my door. "Your rent is late."

"That's the nice thing about bills," I observed. "If you forget to pay them, they always remind you." I took the notice and put it on the counter with the others. We began to chow.

"You haven't been taking many shifts at work," K.J. said.

"That's the nice thing about shifts. No matter how many you take, there's always more."

"Existential S.O.B."

Was that existential? I should know that, shouldn't I?

He continued, "I love pizza and beer. You know what I mean? I *love* pizza and beer. Just *love* it. Know what I mean?"

"What do you mean?"

"I have to laugh—ha, ha—when everyone raves about gourmet foods, caviar and such. You know why?"

"Pray tell."

"'Cause I *love* pizza and beer. You know why more people eat pizza than caviar?"

"'Cause it's cheaper?"

"No, because it's better. And it's because it's better that it's cheaper. See if you can follow this, Mr. Nietzsche. At some point in the past, people—our forefathers, if you will—had a choice between pizza and caviar, right? Now, if caviar was actually better than pizza, demand would have been strong enough that market efficiencies would have brought about methods of production, harvesting and propagation that would have made the price of Beluga plunge. Didn't happen. Why? Because even back then they knew pizza was far superior. Yes, my son, even as we chew, we are reaping the benefits of our forefathers exceptional taste. I'm thinking of writing a paper on it: Toward a Free Market Interpretation of Pizza Price Structure."

"You're giving me chills."

I related the Sarah incident/calamity/tragedy to him. "I tell you, those two could have been Sumo wrestlers," I concluded.

"I thought that was Japanese?"

"Cut it out." I faked sensitivity, but he knew there was no line he couldn't cross. Still, he honored my request by getting semi-serious.

"So it's over with Sarah now. Finally. For sure. That's good. Isn't it?"

"Yeah, well, no. There'll be the repercussions."

"Isn't that an oldies band?"

"This is going to get back to my folks. What's worse, it will reach them through Sarah's folks, which they will consider humiliating. A dishonor. The Old Man will have kittens. I have humiliated not only my family but the whole community."

"It's regulations," K.J. upped the mockery ante. "It's in the Grosse Pointe Korean Community Code of Conduct. No member of the Grosse Pointe Korean Community may break up with another member of the Grosse Pointe Korean Community. Not without signed consent from the

Chamber of Commerce. Article 10 Section 3a. I know you don't like it but without that, total anarchy," he said, shoving an especially cheesy slice into his mouth.

"Look, this is a little bigger than ditching a glutton at breakfast. This is just not done. We have business dealings with Sarah's family. That's a cement bond. I'm doomed. Then I still have to fess up about changing majors."

"Cool, just like on M*A*S*H. Frank Burns to Charles Emerson Winchester III. But you can't let it go till the fourth season."

"I'm waiting for the right time."

"Is that like waiting for the right time to drink that cup of hemlock?"

"Exactly."

"You can still back out. Patch things up with Sarah. It'll be OK, I bet."

"Don't think it hasn't occurred to me. But these last few weeks have been the best of my life. If I back out now I'll be a defeated and broken man for the rest of my pathetic years on this stinkin' Earth. This is it."

"Then let me ask you a question? It might be kind of personal. Do you think Sarah would go out with me?" The carbonated pop of the beer he was opening broke my momentary state of shock.

"What?"

"What what?"

"Are you serious?"

"Yeah."

"My life is in mortal danger and you're thinking about chicks."

"You say that like it was bad. Look you know how hard it is for me to get a decent woman in a non-vegetative state to go out with me. She's on the rebound so maybe this is a good bet. You could be a little more supportive."

"What about...?"

"Toni," he said, irked by my reminder.

"...Toni."

"Just insurance; a back-up option"

"No. The answer is no. I don't think Sarah would go out with you. Remind me never to discuss my woman problems with you again."

"You don't have woman problems. You think you do, but you don't. You've never had a woman problem. To put it all in perspective, let me remind you of The Night of the Finger Puppets."

He had me there. Apart from K.J. and the female specimen directly involved in The Night of the Finger Puppets, I was the only one who knew of that terror-filled evening. We both observed a moment of silence to acknowledge that my experiences with females were pedestrian by comparison and to offer reassurance that the details of that horrifying night would never be revealed. We quickly recovered.

"So what about this girl...?" I asked.

"Toni," he sighed.

"Yeah, Toni. When do we meet?"

"Let's double this weekend."

"Can't. Got a thing with Naomi and everyone. Next weekend for sure."

"That's the thing about weekends--"

I frisbeed a pepperoni at him before he could finish. Like magic, I had a lighter load.

APPLE PIE

SEVENTEEN

The voyage to The Living End Music Festival began innocuously enough. We gathered at Naomi's place—Me, Naomi, Julian, Doobie, Ronnie and Odium—and were all looking forward to heading south for some warmer weather. True, it was only an eight-hour drive, but the forecast for Knoxville was seventy degrees as opposed to about three, which was the temperature in Ann Arbor at four A.M. when we were getting ready to leave. There was a normal amount of milling about, waiting for the stragglers, formulating eating and sleeping plans (it was to be an overnighter), and an on-going Chinese fire drill to get the six of us and our bags into an ancient Toyota Corolla hatchback that hadn't seen a car wash since the Carter administration. It was decided that I would drive first when Naomi said I would and no one protested. Then we were off—almost. We had made a good fifty yards of progress when we realized we had left Odium standing at the curb, like a discarded waxen mannequin. I crunched the car into reverse and rewound back to her position. No amount of pleading had any effect, we implored her to get in but she didn't seem to hear us. Finally, with assured distinction, Naomi said, "Would you get in the car, please?" Odium piled in and we were off in earnest.

Along the way we made a stop at a dingy little grocery store for food, or at least substances that past as such. I had been harboring the idea that these people were the organic gourmet types, confining themselves to mineral water, whole-wheat based snack crackers and various forms of mulch. That they would touch meat or dairy was unimaginable. Wrong. There were no such pretensions evident in their shopping habits. I grabbed one of the little red baskets and everyone darted off to find something to fill it. As expected, no animal flesh was selected, but most of what was could only marginally be considered organic. Ronnie's choice was Little Debbies. He declared them to be absolutely divine and I had to bite my tongue. Julian picked out a huge bag of pretzels, mustard and garlic flavored. "No fat," he said. Odium's choice was an economy sized jar of olives and three Milky Ways. Doobie chose an extra large box of Hostess Twinkies. "Won't boge your high like the MREs in 'Nam. Booby traps and so forth, if you know what I mean." I didn't. In the interests of everyone I filled up a couple of plastic bags with fresh fruit.

APPLE PIE

Then, strangely, everyone was gone. I made my way to the cashier and paid for the whole mess myself. Well, I figured, we'll just settle up afterwards. Right.

I ended up driving the rest of the way, which didn't exactly jibe with the spirit of egalitarianism, but it was just as well. I didn't trust any of them to drive and as driver I had a modicum of space allocated to me alone whereas they were forced into a sardine-like coziness. I now realize the chauffeuring honor had been bestowed upon me as a silent acknowledgement that I was the only one of us who could be described as anything approaching mature or responsible. It only became seriously annoying for a stretch of time when we were lost in southern Ohio and I had to put up with Ronnie's backseat editorializing: "I can't believe we're lost. Oy.", "I'm dead meat if these rednecks get to me. Oy.", "Garland would just die if he knew about this. Oy.", "Oy, can't read a map? Oy.." There was something very disquieting about a portly black homosexual who had affected the Yiddishism "Oy," but that would have been too insensitive and prejudicial to point out.

At last, we pulled into a sea of tightly parked cars in an expansive open field and took directions from a series of diffident orange vested attendants until we were finally guided into a parking space. Groaning in relief like a pack of geriatrics who had simultaneously struggled to stand erect, we vacated our rolling iron maiden.

"Where's the stage?" I asked an orange vest.

He pointed in the general direction of crowd movement. "A little less than two miles. That'll be seven dollars for parking."

I looked around but everyone was already trudging off stage-way. So, again, I dug into my wallet.

The crowd had reached the point of coalescence but the show hadn't yet started. The stage was filled with overfed roadies, randomly repositioning equipment. We identified a landmark and agreed to meet there once the music started, then we split up, each of us with our own agenda—Doobie in search of mind-altering chemicals; Julian to find those carrying demeanors of political correctness and talk about how he was back from the rainforest; Ronnie to cruise for boys, I assume; Odium to find new and different things to fix her vacuous stare on; and Naomi and I to stretch our legs.

We walked along the outer edge of the crowd, our path roughly tracing an impossibly long line of people extending beyond sight in both directions.

After the claustrophobic ride down I was finally beginning to relax, allowing my thoughts to settle on Naomi's ethereal beauty and how thrilling it was to have her hand gripped in mine and how I could just pick up and drive across country at will without worrying about any mispropriety. Naomi, in sync with my thoughts, was saying how wonderful it was to be on this little adventure and how I never would have done something like this a few months ago, when a confused looking proto-human in a Greek-letter sweatshirt fell to his knees in front of us and began asking questions. At least I assumed they were questions from the intonation since not a single syllable was coherent. This random driveling continued for a few moments while Naomi kept asking him what he was trying to say, as if he were susceptible to reason. The torrent of babble finally ended when he began to upchuck a half digested concoction of Reese's Peanut Butter Cups, some unidentifiable form of lunch meat, and what must have been an entire bag of Cool Ranch Doritos. I was not so much disgusted as annoyed with him for interrupting my reverie. We left him to purge in peace, and as we walked on I tried to recapture the above mentioned serendipity but I kept getting distracted by little things— people laughing too loud, people walking across our path, and people standing in that interminable line. What was the deal with that?

"Oh look." Naomi led me to a kiosk where a chubby, scraggly-bearded vendor had tee-shirts hanging on display. There were the standard shirts with the logos of the various bands that were scheduled to play, for which black seemed to be the preferred color, and a smattering of others with trite bumper-sticker phrases on tie-dye. What struck me was the absence of any buyers despite being surrounded by people caught up in the spirits so adequately expressed by them. Not only that, you would have thought, given his considerable inventory, that he could have found one that adequately covered the lower half of his beer-gut.

He was also a little too pleased at the sight of Naomi with one of the shirts draped across her chest.

"Cool, isn't it?" she said as she turned to show me. It said: Make a Living, Not a Killing.

"Very nice."

"This would be great."

The way she said that left no options. If it was a request for purchase, it would be a further strengthening of the bond between us—correctly interpreted innuendo is the mark of a truly connected couple. If it was not a request but merely an innocent expression of desire, then the purchase would be just another sign of my affection and generosity. Either way, major points for me.

"Let's get it," I offered.

"Oh no. You don't have to."

The perfunctory quality of her voice told me I had achieved correctly interpreted innuendo. "I want to. Go ahead."

"You're so sweet."

She kissed my cheek and slipped it on over the tee-shirt she was already wearing. Then, through a stunningly graceful, and more than a little erotic, contortion she removed the original shirt from beneath. It was an impressive display of flexibility that was not lost on the vendor, judging from his leer. I put an end to that with a sharp "How much?"

"Twenty-five dollars."

"No, just the one."

"Twenty-five dollars."

I don't know whether that was the real price or he just knew he had me. There was no time to force the issue because one of the bands had started playing and Naomi said, "Come on, hurry up. They're starting."

I must have visibly blanched when I looked in my wallet because the scum-bag vendor said, "Visa, Master Card, or American Express."

Lucky for me I had one of the Old Man's credit cards. As we left, I finally spotted the end of that inexplicable line. It was a solitary port-a-potty.

EIGHTEEN

I made a mental note to look into lip reading. We had cleverly selected a huge speaker tower as the landmark for our meeting place and I couldn't follow the conversation, my hands over my ears. I tried to listen to the band, Impaled Bob. No, really. I had heard their CD at one of the parties. I didn't like them, but at least I recognized their recording as a sound remotely resembling music. Live, they seemed to eschew any of the generally accepted attributes of music—melody, rhythm, tone, etc.—instead choosing spastic thrashing and aimless howling as their mode of expression. I later learned this was a style called Techno-Goth-Industrial, a term I simply must work into my next poem. Intermittently, someone would touch me on the shoulder to get my attention and ask me a question to which I could only respond "Wha?" followed by a shrug when they rolled their eyes at me. Existence itself seemed to quiver with each thud of the bass drum, causing my sight to go in and out of focus in time with the beat; not that there was any discernible time to the beat. Nor was their much to focus on, the stage being about five hundred yards away.

It occurred to me that no one could possibly be enjoying this. There was simply no pleasurable activity going on here. None of my senses were being favorably affected, nor could I imagine any reasonable person who might feel otherwise. As a distraction, I tried to imagine what the others saw in this endeavor that so enamoured them. If it wasn't directly pleasurable there must have been some intangible benefit, some positive sensation or rewarding conception that they got out of it. It wasn't a sense of accomplishment; it took nothing except my money to get everyone here. And there didn't seem to be any noble moral end in sight, although if pressed, I'm sure Julian could have concocted one. I looked at my new friends one by one, scrutinizing their posture and expressions for a clue. That's when I saw that they were as bored and bothered as I was; they just hid it better. They'd drift into a glassy-eyed state then quickly snap to a stance of riveted attention for as long as they could, as if suddenly remembering that they were supposed to be having a great time. As I saw them go through the same transformation one by one, I came to an important realization: They were posing.

A cold slap in the face prevented me from pursuing that line of thought, delivered by a ferociously violent cloudburst that appeared out of nowhere and gave the impression it intended to stay awhile. People were scattering in all directions. There was the crackle of equipment shorting out on stage, causing Impaled Bob to squeal like a stuck pig. We all looked at each other and started sprinting back to the car. We got back only to discover we were parked in. I looked around for an orange vest to rail at but none were to be seen. There was no other shelter nearby and nowhere else to run.

So began the most excruciating night of my life. Having survived it I am fully confident in my ability to survive an extended stay in a third world prison should the need ever arise. Soaked and sweaty from our forced retreat we had to huddle into the little hatchback and hope the rain would stop soon. It didn't. Throughout the evening hope for a quick end to the downpour slowly dwindled as a creeping nausea slowly grew. I tried to keep a small spot on the windshield free from breath fog in a vain effort to see an end to the storm or just remind myself that there was a world outside the confines of my prison. At least we didn't starve. We amply fed our nausea on the junk food we—I—had purchased. Wind was broken on several occasions, silently, for which I was grateful, and prompted no reaction, for which I was grateful, even though it was obvious, for which I was not so grateful.

For the most part, there was no conversation. The only extended speaking came at dusk when Ronnie got started on Garland. It turns out this Garland character was a some kind of porno king. He "performed" in hundreds of those grainy home video-quality porn flicks that you can order from the backs of certain magazines, ten tapes for twenty dollars or so (I hear). All along, what he really wanted to do was direct. Anyway, this Garland apparently so completely burned out on sex with women that he turned to sex with men. It was a badge of honor for Ronnie that he was the one who finally got Garland to "settle his calepidgeon self down." Keeping an open mind about all that was a struggle. It was not disgust that I was feeling. Well, it was, but that was not the primary source of my negative reaction. It was pity. I don't think I can imagine a more pathetic situation than this guy Ronnie, a basically amicable and intelligent guy, who had so thoroughly screwed up his life and was proud of it. He felt as if everything was peachy as a picnic. He was right where he wanted to be, living life to the fullest. Even if you accept his homosexuality as valid, which I'm not sure I do except maybe in theory, his pride in conquering some third rate skin flick "actor" was nothing short of personal degradation. I guess that makes me insensitive. So, when stranded in detestably close quarters with a bunch of sweaty, smelly people I don't even like to begin with, I'm insensitive. Sue me. The only times I had a chance to breath freely were the three times over the course of the night I ran to the nearby trees to answer the call of nature. Each time I stayed out in the rain for as long as I possibly could, until the drenching became unbearable. Finally we all fell asleep, not so much because we were tired, but as a defense mechanism against the ongoing torture. Or maybe it was lack of oxygen.

I awoke the next morning to find that some sadistic bastard had twisted my spine into a Möbius strip, tied my legs into a perfect double four-in-hand, and had a vice clamped firmly to my shoulders and was torquing it tighter with all his might. My first thought was to escape, but even thinking of moving made the pain worse. I managed to work a hand free and open the door. In slow motion, I eased myself out of the car and achieved a wobbly, but erect, position. In perfect mockery of the night before, the morning was quite lovely—sun beaming, a cloudless sky. I gingerly stretched my limbs and began to entertain the notion that things may be looking up when I made the mistake of taking a step. Flat on my back in a mud bog, I remembered, oh yes, it had been raining. I teetered back to my feet only to fall again, this time on my face. I lay still for a moment and devised a strategy of crawling to the car and pulling myself up by the door handle. That worked fairly well and it would have been an end to it if Doobie hadn't picked that instant to make his exit swinging the door wide and propelling me a good three or four feet into the air and onto my back again. He looked down at me, muttered something about Charlie using the mud for camouflage, and then strode erratically off to the trees. The fact that he could walk unaffected through the mire without slipping, in spite of his drug-addled motor skills, was both curious and annoying.

I had reached the point where I was quite comfortable sitting in the mud and was entertaining thoughts of staying there for a few weeks until it dried up. The others began piling out, groaning and stretching. Julian looked down his pointy little nose at me as if I was just being obnoxious. Naomi gave me one of her wry smirks and said, "You poor thing." Ronnie said, "Well, I've never tried that, at least not at this hour." To further my humiliation, none of them experienced any problems negotiating the mud bog.

I looked to my left and saw Odium. An aura of reverence washed over her face at the sight of me. She dropped to her stomach and began wallowing about like a poet in the mud. When she got herself as filthy as I was she stood up and preened, as if to say, "Great idea!"

The atmosphere improved only marginally on the trip back. At the halfway point we pulled into a gas station where I pumped while the others made for the restrooms. I didn't even bother to look for contributors, I just paid, but when we got back on the road I said, "Gas sure is expensive out here." There was no response.

At the end, even though I acknowledged the whole trip as a disaster, I harbored some small hope that maybe someday I would look back on it and laugh about it. Nope. My sentiment about that trip remains exactly as it was the minute it was over. Shame. Not shame at my behavior, which was above reproach, but shame that I actually bought into the illusion of the romantic bohemian life. I can still recall my epiphany of those people as posers. Well, I took that pose to heart, like some kind of schoolgirl dreaming of Prince Charming. I'm ashamed it took the extremity of that road trip to make me see the truth.

NINETEEN

Anyone who really knows me, and that amounts to about three people, would have given reasonable odds that I would have packed it in and given up at this point, before I had taken any actions that couldn't be reversed or denied. The fuse that was lit by the little girl who could spell had just about reached its end, but I was in too deep to snub it out now.

The term ended uneventfully and Naomi accompanied me to the student bookstore to sell back my accumulated collection of engineering texts. She deemed it to be a symbolic act of rebirth and since she was the vessel of my renaissance—her words, not mine—her attendance was important. The pimple-faced clerk wearing a Star Trek communicator button and pants hanging halfway down his butt was tediously making his way through my old books, looking them up on some sort of price list and recording their value on a calculator. On three separate occasions he accidentally cleared the machine and had to start over, each time slapping himself across the face and saying, "Oh, sorry." Naomi was watching and I twisted my face, intending to indicate what a bizarre creature this was, but she just looked at me with righteous meaning, almost indignantly, as if she was expressing disapproval at my belittling the goon-clerk. I felt small, like a moral leper. I coughed a couple of times to make it look like the face was involuntary. I decided to take the opportunity to bring up the issue of my parents and my fears, where I knew she would be encouraging.

"I'm still not sure I'm ready for this. I can expect to be cut off at a minimum."

"Nobody's ever ready for anything. Look, you don't know what'll happen, you're just worrying for the sake of worrying. Everything will be fine."

"I know what'll happen. I just hope it doesn't ruin me."

"How bad off are you for money?"

"I have enough to register for next term. After that it's a matter of whether I can delay the inevitable long enough. Once the feces hits the fan, I'm going to have to live on tips."

"You're fine then. You see lots of people on the streets that don't have any job and they get by. You shouldn't let money control your happiness. Besides, I think something wonderful is going to happen to you."

"Mmmmm."

We kissed. Her optimism along with a gentle nibble on my ear went a long way toward putting me at ease.

"You know, I feel honored," she said.

"Why?"

"It's like all good teachers say they are honored by their students. Here you are, going through this kind of spiritual awakening and I'm like the doorway to your new awareness. It's very gratifying that you let me do that."

A less love-blind fellow would have choked on the condescension, but to me it was just proof of how devoted and sincere she was.

Apparently there was a malfunction with the communicator because the goon-clerk used the phone to call one of the stockboys over to wheel away my pile of books. "Seven-fifty for the bunch." He counted out my pittance. It worked out to about eight cents a pound and it was to be the last easy money I'd see for...well, forever.

Shortly after registration, K.J. and I were lolling about in my place, lazily tossing around a nerf football.

"We got a class together. Never thought I'd see that," he said.

I had a full set of liberal arts classes; none of which I can name exactly, though most of the titles began with the word Themes, including this one with K.J. which had to do with literary themes of some sort.

An urgent knock at the door filled me with trepidation. It was too strong for Naomi and, with K.J. already present, that left the landlord or worse. It was worse. It was brother George. Feces and fan had intersected. Instantly, I felt a sharp pain in my right eye, like a cold headache, which in retrospect was the correct reaction.

"You dick-head!" he said, opening the conversation. "Oh, hey K.J."

"Hey, Georgie. Good to see you. We were just talking about--" K.J. had to cut short his response, me having whipped the nerf football into his face.

"I can guess what you were talking about," George responded to me. "Mom sent me. She had a talk with Helen yesterday." Helen was Sarah's mom. The pain in my eye spread to my chest. "She said you broke up with Sarah—broke her sweet little heart—for a *blonde* girl. She says, 'George, go talk to your brother. You are the closest to him. Find out what's going on.' You dick-head! You unmitigated dick-head! You know how ashamed Mom must have felt to hear about it from that sacrosanct bitch Helen?"

I knew. Not what sacrosanct meant, but everything else. "Look, I'm sorry to hear about Mom, but it's my business what I do and who I go out with. You don't think she told the Old Man do you?"

"You dick-head! Don't you think the Old Man's gonna find out eventually? What's this?"

He picked up my class schedule and gawked at it, just as I was about to wad it up and swallow it.

"What have you done? What's this crap?"

"Apparently, I've quit engineering."

"Quit engineering?"

"Apparently."

"For what?"

"Apparently, I've become a philosophy major."

"A what?"

"Apparently, I'm going to major in philosophy."

"Apparently?"

"Gimme that." I snatched it back.

"Apparently, you've got a death wish. You must. That's the only explanation."

"Come on, don't tell the Old Man, OK? It'll put me in the acid bath for sure."

"What are you gonna tell him when he sees your degree? They misspelled engineering?"

"I'll tell him eventually, when the time is right."

"You dick-head! You're just gonna drag everyone in with you. Mom already knows about Sarah. She's keeping it from the Old Man for the sake of the peace. Now I know about this. You're gonna pull us all into the acid bath for protecting you."

"Is this guy really that bad?" K.J. asked.

"Worse. I'd rather chew glass than listen to another one of his constipated oratories about discipline and loyalty," I replied.

George agreed. "When I left home for college, instead of the birds and bees lecture, he showed me tricks for solving quadratic equations. Where did you come up with philosophy?"

"I think I'd be good at it."

"The only thing you're good at is rationalizing."

"That's the ticket—law school," K.J. suggested.

APPLE PIE

"You gotta come home and fess up," George demanded.

"I don't gotta do anything. Why do I owe him an explanation? This isn't about him; it's about me. And there's no way I'm going in the acid bath."

"OK. Fine. But he's gonna find out eventually, then you drag Mom and me in with you because we knew and didn't tell."

"You can't hold me responsible for his twisted concept of family values."

"Look, I understand you may have some unresolved issues with me cause I dipped your pig tails in the inkwell when you were a little girl, but Mom doesn't deserve that and you know it. Let's go."

I knew better than to try to fight the mother-guilt. The SOB had me and he knew it. He tossed me my coat and headed out the door. I looked to K.J. for help but he just shrugged. The pain in my chest spread to my gut.

George had managed to combine a sneer, targeted disdainfully at my choice of majors, and a smile, over the prospect of me replacing him in the Old Man's dog house, into an obnoxious leer that was more than a little evil. On the bright side, the effort it took for him to maintain the delicate balance of that expression prevented him from speaking, so we had a silent ride back to Grosse Pointe. I wouldn't have been much for conversation anyway. My thought paths led uniformly to my upcoming acid bath. There was no way to avoid it, never mind turn it around to my favor. And it was going to be the worst ever, administered with a steel wool loofa.

The sight of the hallowed homestead brought no comfort this time. It had taken on the form of a haunted house—icy winds, creaking doors, cobwebs, demons lurking about. The older sibs, Darren and Penny, were over for dinner and it seemed darkly appropriate that my impending immolation would occur in the presence of the entire family. Everyone was gathered in the sitting room. Yes, my ancestral Grosse Pointe home has a sitting room. Not that you can't sit in other areas of the house, but in the sitting room one sits with the intent that something of significance should come of it. In that sense, it's similar to the bathroom.

I hesitated just long enough outside the entrance to compel George to give me a shove in. He walked in past me and sat down, still wearing his perfectly honed leer. Mom's face showed a flash of pain at the sight of me—I suspect it was what her face must have looked like during my birth—but quickly caught herself and fell back into her loving mother role.

Other than an apprehensive glance at George a few minutes later, she didn't —and never has—expressed any displeasure with me over the Sarah incident. You see? A saint I tell you.

"It's so good to see you! You look thin. Have you been eating well?" my mom asked. I just grinned and gave her a peck on the cheek. Then she continued to no one and everyone, "It's just so nice to have the whole family together."

"Alex, you should congratulate your sister. She just performed her first heart transplant," the Old Man announced.

I gave her my sincerest smile. No doubt it was a flawless operation, although she'd never profess any pride in it.

"No, it is Father who should be congratulated. He has just won the Grosse Pointe Chamber of Commerce Symbol of Success Award," said sister Penny, kissing the Old Man on the cheek.

"It was a good choice. After all, we all owe our achievements to Father. If anyone knows about success, it is him." That was Darren. Unlike George, who sucks up to the Old Man out of self-interest, Darren does it simply because it is his nature.

Frankly, I found the proceedings just a little too rich to be believable. I closed my eyes and tried to convince myself it was all a dream—nay, a nightmare. But when I opened them, four Rolexs simultaneously caught the light and reflected it to my eye.

"I propose a toast to Father, who made all our successes possible," said George, his nose a distinct shade of brown. How bad was it? I would have paid good money to be at a poetry reading instead of this.

You'd never find Be Bim Bop being served at our house. We're Americans. We have meat loaf, mashed potatoes, and corn-on-the-cob. This being my last meal, I dug in with gusto. I managed to get a full round of all courses and loaded up for seconds when, "Well, Alex, did you succeed in Thermodynamics last term?"

I was oddly calm. The pain that had been touring my body was gone. I'm not sure why, but it was probably just resignation to my fate.

"Uh, I dropped Thermodynamics."

The Old Man hit me with a look of stoic surprise, which for him was the equivalent of "WHAT!" I got the same reaction when I was six and accidentally left my sweater at school and it was gone the next day. Everyone else stopped not talking and got silent. At times like this, I knew the only thing that could make it worse for me, if that was possible, would be equivocate or obfuscate and force him to draw the truth out of me through interrogation, so I went all the way before he could respond with more than his look.

"You see, I've decided to change my major."

"You're not going to be an engineer?"

"No. I've decided to major in philosophy."

Mom, Darren and Penny cringed. George was displaying mock surprise. The Old Man just tightened his lips.

I had adopted a confident, casual, small-talk tone of voice. I may have been hoping that if I reacted under the guise of ignorance, as if I didn't know it was such a big deal, his hostility would be mitigated. Stupid move; he thought I was belittling the whole thing.

"And you did this without consulting me? You must be joking, eh? Why didn't you discuss this?"

"There really wasn't anything to discuss. I know my feelings..."

"What was it about engineering you didn't like?"

"I don't know specifically. I just felt stifled and claustrophobic."

"Stifled and claustrophobic?" The Old Man almost achieved sarcasm there.

"I can't explain. I just know it's not for me."

"No? It seemed to be *for* your brothers."

"Well, I'm not my brothers." That was the best I could do. I should have brought to his attention that Darren was about as nondescript as a speed bump and George was a pathetic butt-kisser. But at least they were engineers.

"What do you expect to do with a philosophy degree?"

"I don't know yet."

"You don't know."

"I'm not sure. Maybe teach. Maybe write. I haven't figured it out yet. I just know I feel a lot better about this than engineering."

"And what does Sarah think about this?"

Mom braced herself. There was some comfort to be gained from this question; at least I could get Mom off the hook easily. I stopped chewing and looked up, hoping to impress him with my resolve.

"I'm not seeing her anymore."

This caught the Old Man off guard, but only for a second. He quickly identified that as the smaller of the issues confronting us and went back to the main point.

"But you're a senior already. Won't you have to stay in school longer?"

"Yes. But what's the point of graduating on time if I'm going to end up in a job I don't like? Why rush into unhappiness?"

"I see. Have you figured out how *you* are going to pay for this extra schooling?"

He had me there.

My silence prompted his summation. "I just don't understand this. Look around you Alex, look at Penny and your brothers. Are you trying to tell me they have missed something or that they are really unhappy? It's important for me, for the whole family, that you succeed. That is the reason I brought my family to this country so many years ago. All the effort. All the sacrifice. And now you decide you know better—that you know what's for the best and we don't understand. And what's worse, you don't consult, you just defy me."

The last sentence actually brought a raised voice, a rarity. It was punctuated by him throwing down his silverware and pushing his plate away in anger, a first. The meal was over. He rose.

"I am *very, very* disappointed."

Then he left. There was a good two minutes of silence as the shock settled in, then Mom and Penny started clearing the dishes.

George couldn't resist. "I thought that went rather well."

To his credit, Darren slapped him upside the head.

APPLE PIE

TWENTY

Under the illusion that they could talk some sense into me, Darren and Penny decided to drive me back to Ann Arbor with as little delay as possible.

They sat prim, proper, and upright in the front seat of Darren's Oldsmobile, while I slouched across the back. Surviving the confrontation with the Old Man gave me a rebellious rush. My mood was a combination of relief and defiance. I saw the whole mess as a victory. I didn't cave or evade. I stuck to my guns. I was in the acid bath but it didn't matter. I was heading back home where I would sleep without the twin terrors of Sarah and the Old Man to vex me for the first time in months. Sleep next to Naomi. I even felt a hint of perverse pride in prompting such a dramatic response. I made the Old Man get sarcastic, raise his voice, and vent his anger on innocent utensils, all in a span of less than three minutes. That was an unprecedented achievement. What a powerful character I was! Darren and Penny were doomed.

Darren was named after Bobby Darin, who had a big hit on the charts when the family arrived in the U.S. and Penny was named after the character on *Lost in Space*. These were their American names as chosen by the Old Man. They were doomed from the start.

"You have to accept that Father doesn't see things the way we do." Darren said, as if he and I saw things the same. Hah.

"No. Really?"

"You know what I mean. You weren't born in Korea, even the others are too young to remember, but I do. Father used to work in a little grocery store all day and when he got home he would rarely even stop to eat before leaving to work most of the night as a janitor in an office building--"

"I know, I know. And he used to walk to school in his bare feet, in the snow, uphill both ways."

"Don't get cute," he snapped, gazing at me in the rearview mirror. "Just shut up and listen. From the time I was born he's devoted every waking minute to improving our lives. You see these houses and this fine neighborhood, that's what means his life hasn't been in vain. That's the measure of his worth. And now you've just said you think it's meaningless. What did you expect?"

"I expected exactly what I got. And I've got nothing against living well. Where did that come from? I want to live as well as anybody. I just can't do it his way. I'm sorry I wasn't born in Korea and that I can't understand him and all that...no I take that back, I do understand him. He wanted to change his life for the better and so do I."

"But to him you're going backwards. He can't see--"

"This is not about him. Maybe he should try to understand me."

Darren drives slowly. A good five to ten under the speed limit as a matter of principle. As a result, he gets flipped off a lot, but it seems to have no effect on him. On this occasion, he slowed down so much at a turn that the guy behind us thought he was stopping and pulled out to pass just as Darren went into his turn. Brakes squealed and my teeth clenched, but the guy managed to stop short of hitting us. He promptly directed a rather robust double handed bird at Darren. Come to think of it, Darren may not know what that gesture means.

"Why are you turning here?" Penny inquired.

"By taking this route we avoid one stop light."

"But we add a stop sign," she challenged.

"A stop sign is preferable to a stop light. You don't have to wait so long," Darren countered.

"Unless the light is green," Penny persisted.

"If you assume the light is going to be green fifty percent of the time and red fifty percent of the time, as long as you don't stop at the sign for half the length of a red light, you come out ahead at the stop sign."

"That also assumes you have to stop for the full duration of the red light. What about the times when you get there and it has already been red a while."

"If you assume--"

"OK, stop. Just stop it now," I interrupted. God help me. How was I supposed to live a life—a free life—in their world?

It was Penny's turn to take a shot at me. "I don't want to take sides Alex, but this is very strange. You've never expressed any interest in philosophy before."

"There's a lot you don't know about me."

"You know, Father's right about your future. There's not a lot you can do with a philosophy degree. At least not that will make you a living."

"You mean I should be more practical, maybe devote myself to solving the great stop light vs. stop sign debate?"

"When did you get so sarcastic? I know it seems like what direction you pick now is going to define you, but it's not." She fidgeted—another first. "I've never told anyone this, but do you know what I do in my spare time? I write children's books—illustrate them too."

There was a slight pause as Darren and I digested that.

She continued, "You see, I have plenty of money so that gives me the opportunity to do whatever I want with my spare time. There's nothing to tell you what to do when you get home. If you want to study philosophy you can, and you still have your good job and your good income. There's a lot to be said for not having to worry about money."

"There's a big difference, though. You enjoy medicine, and you enjoy engineering. I don't. I don't want to spend a huge part of my life doing something I hate--"

Darren had heard enough. "You just think you are so smart! You think you've got everything figured out, but you aren't looking past your penis!"

Whoa. That was a big first. No one in my family ever used that word.

"What?" I replied. And besides, how did he know about Naomi?

"You heard me."

"Kindly leave my penis out of this. Look you guys, I have given this a good deal of thought over the last...well, my whole life. I'm not doing anything wrong. Wasn't there a time when you wanted to be irresponsible, romantic, follow your heart, just enjoy the moment for a change instead of worrying about the future? And Darren, you don't have to stop at a yield sign. It'll screw up your assumptions."

APPLE PIE

TWENTY-ONE

Again, a hard won victory didn't quite live up to its billing. Having survived the inescapable confrontations with Sarah and the Old Man, however haphazardly, the cord to my past was finally cut clean through and I should have been walking on air. A month previous I would have been in ecstasy, but I was disillusioned with my new crowd—a persistent hangover from the disastrous road trip—and I was starting to entertain notions that it hadn't been worth it after all.

My heightened cynicism spilled over into my relationship with Naomi. During one evening study session, which meant she was engaged in an extended monologue, the topic of materialism came up. I took the opportunity to bring up my financial situation and explained to her how low I was on money and that I had some rough times ahead. I wasn't looking for a loan (or even a reimbursement), all I was hoping for was some understanding and sympathy. She didn't catch on.

"...it's the utter rejection of the material way of life. The social aesthetes know that society is either totally non-materialistic or totally materialistic. There's no in-between. You can't have some materialists and some non-materialists because the materialists will impoverish the non-materialists."

"I don't know, there's a lot to be said for the importance of material things. After all, food is material, clothing is material, so are tee-shirts and gasoline." I couldn't resist that little dig. No use, she was lost in the theoretical.

"No. Don't you see? Those things only become important to you when they're someone else's property. Food is a concern because someone else owns it and won't give it up without a profit."

I got more direct. "My dad has cut me off. I don't know how I'm going to keep up with rent, never mind tuition. I needed his material to live and do what I wanted. Now it's gone. I can't just pretend to be above it."

"Yes that's it! The money is important to your father. It's his property and as a result you have no choice but to be materialistic too."

"You seem to have missed your cue," I intimated. "We're not talking about philosophy class anymore. This is real. This is my life. I have to deal with it every second of every day. I can't afford to be so impractical."

"Are you saying you're going to give in to your father?"

"I don't know." A lie. I did know. I would never give in. If not out of principle, out of pride, or perhaps spite. "I'm saying I'm going to have to make some choices, some seriously ugly choices. This is just not working out the way it was supposed to."

"What's come over you? I really thought you were getting over being so reactionary."

"Reactionary? I suppose I'm an enemy of the oppressed too."

"You know what I mean. You've been sullen and anti-social. You were like that on the trip back from The Living End. You've been doing so well at getting beyond all that baggage. Don't struggle against the opening of your mind..."

I don't remember too much from basic chemistry, but if I had to take a shot at the densest element, I would guess Naomium. I was close to an explosion and it must have shown in my face because she ceased her polemic and took up a conciliatory tone. She touched my cheek and slipped an arm around me.

"You know what the only absolute truth in the universe is? 'This too shall pass.' Try not to worry so much, OK?" she said with an angelic smile.

I took a deep breath and cautiously decided to withhold my reaction. She did have a way of calming me and making it seem like everything was going to be fine. We shared a look that made it clear that our little exchange was no big deal, just the result of me being on edge, and there would be no lasting effects to us. But that was the first time I ever walked away from sex with her. I just wasn't in the mood. My attitude did improve, and within a couple of days we were back to normal, but the incontrovertible fact of the money thing lingered.

The exact title of the class I shared with K.J. was Themes of Social Literary Interpretation in the Modern Era. You guessed it: SLIME. It was taught by a short, middle-aged, somewhat cocky geezer with a bold, Roman nose and deep-set eyes. He had a well-practiced crooked smile under a salt and pepper goatee that was probably supposed to make him look casual and reassuring. He dressed in the perfunctory corduroys and cardigan. I just knew he had a pipe hidden away somewhere to sneak a puff now and then to create a fatherly impression on his female students.

Shortly before the start of the first class, Julian entered and took a seat in front of K.J. and myself. We exchanged nods of acknowledgement but no words since, although we spent a good deal of time together in other surroundings, we were not all that comfortable with each other in the absence of the party buffers. That is to say, I still didn't like him and he probably knew it. Not only that, I don't think he would have lasted more than three minutes in the leveling wind of K.J.'s sarcasm.

Somewhat implausibly, I had actually done some of the required reading in preparation so I was looking forward to really getting something valuable out of this class. The professor began, employing a resonant, patriarchal, deadly significant baritone.

"Can anyone tell me the relevance of the marlin in The Old Man and the Sea to the lesbian paradigm?"

K.J. and I exchanged looks. Mine confused, his resigned. Julian, naturally, had the answer.

"Clearly, the marlin is the dyke figure and Santiago is the traditional oppressive male. Hemmingway is advocating the false dogma that a male can reform a lesbian through violent means."

"Clearly," said K.J. to me, struggling to keep a straight face.

"It could be valid, I suppose," I said, trying not to struggle against the opening of my mind.

"Very good!" said the professor.

"Welcome to liberal arts," K.J. said, indicating that we may as well use this lecture to quietly hold a more consequential conversation.

"Maybe that's how you should have explained it to your father. 'Dad, I'm afraid engineering isn't relevant to my paradigm.'"

I shrugged in false indifference. "I'm afraid I am fully renounced. Of course I got no help from anyone. You should have heard Darren and Penny, what a couple of hamsters. It's hard to imagine we're from the same gene pool. And you know George."

"OK, here's what you do. You go home tell your folks you have an incurable disease. You only have two years to live so you've decided to ditch the rat race and enjoy your last little time on Earth. Then, once you graduate, you miraculously recover. Too bad about that engineering thing, but it's too late now."

"No chance. A) My sister's a doctor. B) The Old Man would just insist I double my engineering class load to get my Masters before I die an empty, qualitative death."

"Lucky you don't have to deal with that kind of nonsense anymore." K.J. motioned to the professor who had gotten himself so worked up over the topic of his lecture that he was pacing back and forth, waving his arms in grand, dramatic gestures.

"Thus we see that, as a recurring theme, Hemmingway was most certainly no friend of animal rights."

TWENTY-TWO

A couple weeks later, having settled into the routine of my new classes, Naomi and I finally doubled with K.J. and what's-her-name.
I was looking forward to seeing K.J. and the unpredictable experience of meeting someone he's dating. I knew Naomi didn't like K.J. so on the walk over to the restaurant I tried to relate some humanizing story about K.J. to nudge her into a good frame of mind. I had to carefully select my K.J. story because there are so many, some of which I am honor bound not to tell, that she would have seen as evidence of his crudity. I settled on a highly fictionalized version of one from a couple of years ago.
"...so it turns out she had some kind of mental condition. Multiple personality disorder, I suppose. One personality was dating K.J. and the other was some sort of psychotic hedge-trimmer murderer or something, I can't remember exactly. Anyway, it didn't last. She had neglected to shave her legs before one of their dates and K.J., being the most sarcastic man in the world, said, 'Hey babe, don't you know fur is out?' Wrong personality. It took him weeks to get over the haircut."
Naomi was laughing, perhaps a bit too hard. "So this could be an interesting night?"
"At least."
They were sitting at a corner table looking at the menus. Her back was to us and her puffy-permed blonde hair was bobbing in animated conversation. K.J. had this glassy look in his eyes that I knew meant he wasn't paying attention to a word she was saying. As we walked over to the table Naomi whispered, "What was her name?"
"Hi, I'm Toni. With an 'i'. Hee, hee," she introduced herself.
She was pretty enough, in heavy-handed way. What she lacked in grace and refinement she made up for with a sort of glossy youthfulness. She was not so much a girl as a cartoon rendition of one; assuredly a freshman, probably not more than nineteen.
Naomi got us started. "It's nice to finally meet you, Toni. Are you a freshman?"
"Yes. Oh my Gawd! Does it show? I was, like, so nervous about going out with older people."
"Don't worry. We're all friends here."
"I can't help it. I mean, what if I get carded? That'd be so embarrassing. I have a fake ID but it's not very good. Can they arrest you for that?"

APPLE PIE

"They only arrest you for the good ones." Lame humor on my part.

"Cool." She didn't get it. "What can I order that won't be too suspicious?"

"How about a boilermaker?" K.J. said, but he was ignored.

"I can't have anything with sugar. It makes me break out. How about a strawbeery daiquiri? Are those OK?" She actually said strawb*ee*ry, that's not a typo.

Things were going pretty smoothly, the conversation was lively; everyone was demonstrating tolerance for everyone else's little peculiarities and we were finding middle ground subjects that everyone could be involved in for a while. Outwardly, Naomi appeared indulgent of K.J.'s juvenilia (again, her term, not mine) but I sensed her patience was waning.

"I would never give a homeless guy any cash. He'd probably go spend it on cheap wine," K.J. said.

Naomi took that with indigence masked as continuing conversation. "That always seemed to me to be an excuse. What do you suggest he buy?"

"Oh I don't know. Maybe a nice Beaujolais or pouilly-fuissé."

She ignored him and continued indoctrinating Toni, who had become her cause of the moment. "Look, Toni, you don't have to work with the homeless; there are lots of choices, and the best part is you get three sociology credits for it. There's this one program where you go to work in a one-room school in some remote part of Borneo. The indigenous culture is barely out of the stone age. They have this very simple religion where they just worship a generic genderless, deity called the Great One..."

"They worship Wayne Gretzky?" K.J. said. I laughed, hoping nobody saw the shard of ginger and garlic pasta fly out of my mouth.

She ignored him again, but in the nearly indiscernible pause that followed I heard the snap of a toothpick. I realized, and regretted, that I had been laughing at K.J.'s little quips throughout the evening (which, in her words, would be encouraging him).

"Or you could do what I did my sophomore year—work with autistic children."

"Oh wow. Autistic in what way?" Toni confused us all with this question.

"What do you mean? Is there more than one way to be autistic?" Naomi asked.

"I mean did they paint or play piano or what?"

"Not *ar*tistic, *au*tistic, the learning disability."

"Oh. I thought you said artistic and you said autistic." Toni giggled freely at her own bubbleheadedness.

Having settled that little misunderstanding Naomi made a clearly strategic move, although I could not clearly comprehend her strategy.

"So how long have you two been together?" she asked.

"A couple of months, I guess," Toni replied.

"That's nice. So what do you learn from K.J.?"

"What do you mean?"

"I figure women and men get different things from their relationships. Men, I think, want someone who makes them feel special and worthwhile. Women get involved with guys they can learn something from. Don't you think?" Naomi explained, without a hint of cattiness.

"I don't know, I guess so. What do you learn from Alex?" Toni replied.

Naomi took my hand. "We come from very different directions. He came out of a very paternalistic family, very structured and repressive. I've never experienced anything like that at all. I've always pretty much done whatever I wanted. So I'm learning what it's like to be like that and how to get past it. Learning is what makes a relationship intimate."

I didn't take offense at that, even though I probably should have. By taking my hand and giving me a loving look she made it seem like that was just part of our story, our continuing journey, our lore to be passed to posterity. Yuck.

"I don't know." Toni said, chanting her mantra. "I never thought about that. I guess he's just fun to hang out with, you know. He's pretty funny, but smart too, you know. Like a character on a sitcom or something. Oh oh. I have to pee." She giggled.

Naturally, Naomi and Toni left for the restroom together. I was grinning. Partially because I saw such an obvious difference in quality, depth and refinement between Naomi and Toni, and partially I knew it would piss K.J. off.

"What?" K.J. replied to my grin.

"Oh nothing."

"What?" he repeated, this time with a punch to my shoulder for emphasis.

"Nothing!"

"She's got a lot of potential."

"I'm sure she does."
"You never know, she may turn out great."
"You never know."
I knew I got him good 'cause he punched my shoulder again.
"You know what you are? A chucklehead," he snapped.
"A chucklehead?!"
"Definitely a chucklehead."
"Wow, that's a C. Are you calling me a C?"
"I'm calling you a full-on, totally robust, undeconstructed chucklehead."
I chuckled.
"Look at you. Blind as a bat and dense as a brick and you get a girl like Naomi. Ah, well, maybe that's the secret," he said, downing the remnants of his wine.
I found that to be somewhat cryptic, but I continued in form. "No, that's not it." I leaned close and whispered, "It's 'cause of my enormous genitals."
K.J. did a picture perfect spit-take. I almost fell off my chair laughing.
"I'm trying to eat here!"
Then I had to get serious. "Do you think you could pick up the tab tonight? I'm a little short."
"You just said you were enormous."
"Duh. I'll get ya next pay day," I offer lamely.
"Don't worry about it."
"I gotta find some extra income."
"I hear your dad has some. Go back to engineering."
"I have not yet begun to...to...to not be an engineer." The waitress arbitrarily set the check down in front of me. I pushed it over to K.J. "Sorry, man."
K.J. paid up before the women returned, saving me the embarrassment of an explanation.
"Whoa, I'm beginning to feel that wine," Naomi declared.
"Then you better wipe off your fingers. No wait, I forgot; it was dry."
It was more stupid humor from K.J., but we had all had a bit too much to drink. The reaction from Naomi and Toni was what gave me pause. They exchanged a look—a knowing, confirming look—that gave me a flash of insight into their restroom conversation. Through the night, Naomi had built up an image of herself as an adult woman, in contrast to the

inexperienced freshmen Toni, and there was an underlying perception that we, Naomi and I, had some sort of mature relationship that was obviously superior to the superficial one that Toni and K.J. had. She cemented the impression with all that "learning" nonsense, and I just knew she elaborated on the theme when they were in the restroom, quite effectively introducing doubts about K.J.'s merit into Toni's alleged mind. Being a complete waterhead, Toni would probably believe whatever this adult woman said and even be grateful for the wisdom from on high.

I found such vulgar manipulation and vindictiveness utterly reprehensible. On the other hand, K.J. could have gone a little easier on the sarcasm, knowing full well how Naomi can be about her sacrosanct (I looked it up) ideas. Maybe K.J. should have been more circumspect in targeting his flippancy. On the other other hand, a retarded wombat could see that there was no future for K.J. and Toni, so maybe it was no harm, no foul. Or maybe it was nothing but an innocent glance between girls and I was experiencing a mild drunken paranoia. K.J. didn't pick up on it—or at least he didn't appear to—so I let the matter evaporate from my mind.

APPLE PIE

TWENTY-THREE

Things were really kicking into high gear; I mean, in a bad way. I was fighting a losing battle to keep up with my bills by working every extra shift I could get (the Old Man had cancelled my—his—credit card), sometimes skipping class to do so, and I was still barely treading water. Here's how low I sank: I became a professional guinea pig.

I answered this hand written advertisement posted in the student union for a subject in a psychological experiment. The guy running the show was this truly ghoulish looking psych intern. He had a twitchy, otherworldly way of looking about, never quite meeting your eyes, and he spoke with a strained regulation, as if he was measuring every word, trying to not to betray his true identity to the Earthling. The first time I walked into his lab he tossed a red rubber ball at me and before I could say a word he asked me what it was.

"A ball?" I thought it might be a trick question.

"I'm sorry, what did you say?" It sounded like I was being corrected.

"A ball."

"A ball?"

"Yes, a ball. A red rubber ball."

"Ah ha. I see." That exchange seemed to please him and he jotted something on a notepad. He motioned for the ball and I lobbed it back to him.

"This time catch it in your left hand."

I did.

"Quickly! Hide it behind your back!"

I did. "This is pretty str--"

""Sshhh! No words. Now, would you tell me what I just threw you?"

"The same thing."

He arched an eyebrow. "But what would you *call* it?"

"A red rubber ball."

His expression indicated that my response was unexpected. He made a few more notes.

"Did I make a mistake?"

"Oh no. No no no. There are no mistakes. Please sit down. Now, what makes you think you made a mistake?"

"Well, your reaction I guess."

"And what was my reaction?"

"You seemed disappointed."

"Disappointed? You mean when you told me it was a—what did you call it?"

"A red rubber ball."

"Remarkable." He nearly laughed with glee as he set to scribbling again. "Can you be here every Tuesday and Friday at 3:10?"

"Sure." If there's money in it.

"There will be twenty sessions. Each session will last forty-five minutes and you will be paid twenty dollars at the end of each session."

Thanks to the quantitative excellence I had acquired from my engineering training, I knew that was four hundred dollars total. "That's fine. What exactly are you trying to find out with this?"

"Uh-uh! No more questions like that. You just respond, I'll interpret. I'll see you on Tuesday."

He turned his focus to his notes and I vanished from his reality, such as it was. What followed was, twice a week as planned, he placed me in very odd surroundings—inside a cardboard box, standing in a bucket of what appeared to be mud, posed like the Buddha under a strobe light, and a slew of other absurd positions—and he would ask me what it was he tossed to me. Invariably I responded, "A red rubber ball," and he would scribble in his notebook. If I ever go back to school I simply must figure out how to tap into all that grant money.

I must say that the stupidity of the whole thing offended me for a few sessions. At first the whole thing seemed merely an excuse to indulge in some perverted fetish. But in time I decided just to be grateful for the twenty bucks. After all, Guinea pigging is a crapshoot and I could have been involved in some sort of really twisted medical experiment. Or I could have been selling various bodily fluids.

Between Project Psycho, working at the restaurant virtually every night (where I could garbage-mouth the leftovers for sustenance) and staying clear of any more road trips, I was able to keep up on my tuition and pay my rent. The hidden cost was a perpetual state of exhaustion. I fell asleep everywhere—in class, in the library, at the parties, where I could pretend to have passed out from careless indifference, thus impressing everyone with my hip attitude. I didn't know where I was supposed to be half the time and the other half I knew but wasn't there (it makes sense if you think about it). The parties lost their luster. They ceased to be an event of choice but of duty, or perhaps habit. I don't know why I didn't stop going. I guess I just didn't have anywhere else to go and, for better or worse, they were part of my definition now. I was one of them and that's what they did.

The term began to blow by pretty fast. In previous years I had always carried with me a sense of position relative to the school semester. Not that I could tell you exactly how many days were left until finals or anything that detailed, but I always knew whether we were early on in the year, past the middle; just a feel for general positioning. That sense of orientation was replaced by a harried immediacy that made prioritizing a very straightforward matter. I was always doing what needed to be done right now—a shift at work, a Project Psycho session, be at class, study with Naomi, a party—the litany was reordered from time to time, but it never ended. I should have sacked the whole thing right there, dropped out and headed south or something, but I had given up on plans and schemes and entered a sort of survival mode. Just trying to get through things, not day by day, but in roughly ten-minute intervals. Alas, it was my illusions, not my existence, I was trying to keep alive. (Please forgive the alas.) In my more lucid moments I found myself looking forward to the end of the term, thinking it would bring relief. But then what? I couldn't register for next term and there was no way I was going back home to live. Maybe, I thought, a future-less life would be nice for a change.

What's worse, it was a wicked cold winter and it was months without MFG. You would think if I got a break from the madness I would just try to get a good night's sleep, but at my first opportunity I set up an MFG session with K.J. You see, nightmares or loud neighbors would have interrupted sleep, but the combination of the first warm evening of the year and being back at MFG with K.J. was thoroughly replenishing.

"The movie was called what? Three Women Having an Episode?" K.J. asked.

"Three Women of Sanguine Experience. It was very thought provoking," I said in justification.

"Oh I see. So did these women happen to *experience* a lack of clothing? You know, at the same time, together..."

"Only in a valid, aesthetic sense."

"Huh?"

"There was some nudity, but it was for cogent symbolic reasons." I was beginning to worry myself. I thought that up too easily.

"I repeat: Huh?"
"It was artistic."
"Autistic? In what way?"
We chuckled at that. I had neglected to ask about Toni; I assumed it had come to an end a long time ago. I was right.
"She dumped me," He offered.
But I thought he would have dumped her. "No way," I said.
"Yep."
"Toni with an i? How come?"
"I don't wanna tell you."
"Why not?"
"Cuz."
"Cuz why?" This was getting silly.
"Just play," he said, indicating a tree.
"You can tell me. What could be so bad?"
"Just play, woudja?"
I considered letting the subject go, but this was irresistible. He was never afraid to tell me about his break-ups. Not even The Night of the Finger Puppets.
"Was it another guy? No—another girl? No, no wait—a mechanical device?" I pursued.
"None of the above." He tried to grab the frisbee. "I'll go next then."
"C'mon." I held it away.
"You'll make fun."
"When do I ever make fun?"
He tossed a look my way.
"OK, I always make fun. But I won't this time. Or at least I'll try not to."
He sighed. "She said, quote, You fail to challenge me intellectually. I'm just not learning and growing from our relationship."
I confess I guffawed, but caught myself. "Hey man, that's too bad."
"I'm not intellectual enough for Toni with an i. Toni with an i, who wonders why some countries require VISAs but not Master Cards. Toni with an i, who, when I said I enjoyed Chekov's plays, said 'Oh, so you're, like, a big trekkie?' Toni with an i, who thinks Strunk and White must be great fashion designers. This is the girl I don't stimulate intellectually."

I was sick to my stomach over this. I mean, I thought I was going to throw-up if I didn't get to laugh real soon. K.J. noticed and gave me leave. "Go ahead."

After my laughing fit we sat silently for a little while. The memory of Naomi's manipulation, or at least my suspicion of it, came back to me. K.J. and I couldn't discuss whether he actually had feelings for Toni with an i. That would have fallen under the heading of a serious topic, and as such our emotions were only to be interpreted, not stated. But suppose he did have feelings for her, and suppose Naomi was responsible for planting the seed in Toni with an i's mind, if mind is what you'd call it. What did that make me? A false friend? A traitor? And what could I do about it? Confront Naomi? She would tell me she had no idea what I was talking about, which would either be true or unprovably false. Plus, what kind of boyfriend accuses his girl of something on a vague impression? Circumstances had me trapped in a situation I couldn't resolve, just had to endure. My friendship with K.J. would survive, but I think that quiet moment was his way of saying he thought it was Naomi's fault, and though he didn't care a whit about Toni with an i, he thought I should know what kind of woman I was involved with.

My abstract fatalism protected me from feeling too much guilt about it, but it was floating around in the back of my mind for a long time, perhaps generating the same suspicions in me toward Naomi that she may have generated, possibly, for Toni with an i toward K.J. Perhaps, may have, possibly—I might someday be almost vaguely certain of it. Such is the power and perplexity of interpreted feelings.

APPLE PIE

TWENTY-FOUR

As final exams approached, I dug in deeper and focused even more intently on survival. Project Psycho had ended. The parties had become less frequent. I even took a break from work to prepare. I don't know why; it didn't matter. Enrolling for next term was out of the question. It was all a matter of inertia, and escape. As long I stayed busy and kept up a strong, if aimless, momentum, I was able to hang on to a shred of my vision, my beautiful vision of freedom and serendipity that I had embraced what seemed like a lifetime ago. Without that, everything would have been for nothing and I would vanish into non-being.

During one evening's study session with Naomi, I was being what she had called reactionary. What that meant was that I was questioning her assumptions and not quietly acquiescing to her sermonic monologue. She made a disapproving comment about me being temperamental.

"Is it a rule that I have to agree with you?" I asked, being careful avoid sarcasm.

"Of course not. You know better," she said dismissively.

"Good, cuz I don't. Are you sure that's OK? I haven't caused any friction, have I?"

"Alex--"

"I mean, reactionary is another point of view, isn't it?" Sarcasm was beginning to rear its ugly, but practical, head.

"I just meant it's not helpful. Look, there are going to be different challenges with your new life..." That would be the one she was guiding me through like an honored teacher. "...and I don't think you attitude is very constructive to the opening of your mind. We've discussed this before."

This time, the condescension and arrogance hit me like a hard right to the solar plexus from one of Sarah's roommates. I was speechless, which she took to mean that I saw she was right and the matter was closed and she could casually resume her lecture. That probably wasn't any more condescending or arrogant than any number of things she had said before, but that was the one that got to me. I was more or less silent the rest of the night and we did make love, but it was the last time.

There were some things I just could not bring myself to do. I made some compromises that I'm not very proud of. Case in point: in my last

SLIME class of the year, the one with K.J., the topic of our term paper was announced.

"The topic of your term paper is," the Prof. said with a flourish, as if he were introducing a play, "Themes of Pious Oppression in Literature Since 1950." He wrote it on the board so I was forced to believe my ears. He continued, "You must identify at least three such themes from your readings, either explicit or sub-conscious, and explore them fully..."

K.J. hung his head in despair. I had to get out of this. There was no way I was going to write such a paper. I simply could not force myself to do it. Julian was in the row in front of us and I was desperate.

"I'll give you twenty bucks to do my paper," I told him.

K.J. looked at me, shocked.

"Twenty-five—C; Fifty—B; Hundred—A," Julian answered instantly.

I had heard he did that kind of thing, the miserable, hypocritical, amoral, greedy little dirtbag.

"Give me a B."

K.J. was still looking at me, shocked.

"So?" I responded to his look.

"Does he do this often?"

"Yeah. He keeps a database of essays and term papers, mostly adaptations New York Times editorials from the Seventies. It's a booming business, he'll probably have an I.P.O. when finals are over."

K.J. thought for a minute. "I'll take a B too," he told Julian.

Yes it was dishonest, but come on. Themes of Pious Oppression? What does that mean? Would somebody tell me what that means? The more I thought about it, the less guilty I felt. OK, I guess I did regret the dishonesty, but not because I was making myself a cheat and a liar. I regretted it because I did it for no good reason. With my prospects for the future, of what possible relevance was the grade I got in that class? I never would have done anything like that until that year, but I'd come a long way.

The next thing I knew I was at work. I walked up to a table, order pad and pencil primed, introduced myself and recited the specials to a harmless looking older couple who were studying the menus with more than sufficient intent. They refused to acknowledge me and seemed confused and uncomfortable, as older people can in twenty-something Ann Arbor. I put on my best I'm-here-to-help-you expression, but that only seemed to cause them offense. Hushed snickering began to emanate from the other customers. When I scanned the room to see what was going on everyone averted their eyes. The reason was immediately apparent. What was making everyone act so strangely was simply that I was wearing no clothes. Not a stitch. Oddly, the first thing I felt was curiosity. How could I have traveled across campus all the way to the restaurant, past all my co-workers and out on to the floor without noticing that I was bucknaked? Mismatched socks, sure. A popped button—that happens. Even split trousers I could understand, but this was a little over the edge. A practical joke? Had someone snuck up on me and removed all my clothes without my knowing it?

The snickering turned to hooting and catcalls and my curiosity turned to gasping embarrassment. With lightning speed I snatched the menus from the old couple and strategically positioned them to give me the needed cover. I began to stutter an apology but was struck dumb as I noticed that where once sat the harmless old man now sat my SLIME professor. He was wearing a decidedly self-satisfied smirk to show that he was so far above the common folk that my little display was merely amusing to him. That and a full set of clothes. In another odd reaction, instead of surprise at his presence, I wondered if he was here to confront me about cheating.

An even bigger shock was that the harmless old woman had been replaced by Naomi. She rifled a withering how-could-you-do-this-to-me stare at me that shriveled me to the point of making the menus superfluous.

The crowd was now jumping and shouting like it was a professional wrestling match. It was time for me to flee, but again I was shocked in place when, to my horror, Naomi and the man from SLIME had now been replaced. This time it was my parents. Their heads were hung, hands covering their faces, wailing in such agony that I could hear them distinctly above the crowd. Suddenly, out of nowhere, brother Darren appeared. Wearing a serial killer expression (and, yes, a full set of clothes), he leapt upon the table, extended both arms rigidly toward me and, with both hands, displayed the most violent double flip-off conceivable. When I looked around, everyone—the crowd, my parents, Naomi, SLIME-man, the crowd—was doing the same: double-birding me. Unspeakable mortification welled up in my throat and erupted in a searing howl...

I was still screaming when I woke up. I was still screaming even after I realized it was all a dream. I was still screaming because I was late for my last final exam.

My recollection of my crazed rush to class that day is not entirely complete. I can only piece the sequence together from flashbacks that make their way through my defense mechanisms against traumatic memories.

I remember a sickening acidic nausea, as though my stomach was being burned away from the inside by a toxic mixture of bile and adrenaline. I have since learned that it was the beginning of an ulcer.

I'm fairly certain I collided with every stationary object in the apartment because I was thoroughly bruised for the following week. Plus, it's the way I am.

I have a vision of someone chaining his bike to a parking meter—stupidly, because anyone could have just lifted it, lock and all, over the top and carry it off. I assume the vision is a memory since my bike was gone when I went back for it.

I also have the vague impression of being engulfed in the color brown and feeling like a drowning man who is resigned to his fate. I regret not having a video of the fall because I was still cleaning mud out of various orifices two days later so it must have been worthy of a Funniest Home Video grand prize.

As I approached the classroom I quite clearly recalled that I had only attended that class a handful of times; I couldn't even remember the name of it, or the subject for that matter—Themes of something, no doubt. At that realization, I was suddenly back to full consciousness.

I had transformed from teetering madness to sober as a judge in the span of about five seconds. And I stopped just outside the door, frozen in my steps. Trying to breathe was no use. It took more energy to force my lungs to expand than the breath replenished. The possibility of cardiac arrest ran through my mind. In the circumstances, a heart attack may have been a relief, but something more frightening and enlightening struck me—this was the same reaction I had had some months ago. My mind rewound to standing outside Thermodynamics and being unable to force myself to go in. The panic that I felt then was so deep and profound that it changed my life, now it returned for an encore. I was there again—the incessant anxiety, the defeat and helplessness, the little girl who could spell—this was the same reaction.

Suddenly, I became giddy. I knew what this was and, once identified, the terror was rendered impotent. As if I had confronted a shadowy figure in a dark alley only to find it was a trusted friend, my fear and panic vanished. Prosaic; that's the word I want. It felt prosaic. I began to breathe easy. This deep, profound hysteria, worthy of altering my world—it was just life. Everyday ordinary life.

The emotions that overwhelmed me just a few months ago now only induced a shrug. The heart attack I was about to suffer turned into this frivolously ticklish little feeling in my chest. I laughed out loud at the sensation, at my own foolish inconsequence, then casually entered the classroom.

By then, I was about twenty minutes late and all the students looked up as I entered, perfectly choreographed; their slack-jawed gazes fixed on me. I almost said, "What? Did I fart or something?" Instead, gave them a what-are-you-looking-at face in return. When that had no effect, I did say it. That put them back to work.

The professor here was a sour-faced old crone of imperious visage, who I half expected to berate me for the consummate decline of humanity since the Victorian age. Instead, she sniffed indignantly and handed me a copy of the test as I walked past her to find a seat.

The next issue that arose was my lack of paper. Apparently, the matron felt we would be so honored to be taking her test that we would gladly bring our own paper. I resented being required to provide the vessel of my own destruction. "Oh, I'm sorry. How stupid of me to think we would be provided paper? I realize you're far too busy passing judgement on ruffians and smiting ne'er-do-wells to design your test with space for our answers. I'll just pop out and buy a ream. Won't be a moment. Is there anything I can do for you while I'm out? Get your car washed? Do your laundry, perhaps?"

I teetered on the brink of saying that too, but then I noticed that the ghastly looking greaseball sitting next to me had actually lugged a ream in, just in case he decided to rewrite *Remembrance of Things Past* for one of the answers.

"Pssst. Pssst," I targeted a whisper at him. His head snapped around and he looked at me like I had just insulted his mother.

"Do you suppose you could loan me few sheets of paper?"

It wasn't really a loan I guess, since there was no way I was going to track this guy down later and return his few sheets of paper, but I figured the facade of fair dealing would help my cause.

He cocked his head and thrust his upper lip at me in disbelief, then forked over a small stack of the paper. But there was yet another issue to address. I searched my pockets and realized I had no pen.

Without looking, and thoroughly amused by my own predicament, I knew my greaseball buddy would have an extra pen. If the guy brought an entire ream of paper just to be on the safe side, it was a good bet he was packing about thirty writing utensils of various species. One glance told me I was right. I paused for a moment, just to revel in the absurdity of the situation.

"I say old boy, do you suppose I could touch you for a pen also?" The English accent was sauce for the goose.

I got exactly the same upper class Twit-of-the-Year look and, as a bonus, an unmistakable click of the tongue. He handed over a pen and I proceeded to set down some of the most portentous BS ever set down on borrowed paper.

When the test was over I felt a deep desire to shout, "I love it!" So, again, I did.

TWENTY-FIVE

And that was that. School was over and I was left with some thinking to do. It took only a moment to realize my newfound view of all this nonsense as prosaic did not extend to Naomi. No way did I view her with the same jaded cynicism that I looked on the rest of my life. We had had some problems of late, mostly because I was no longer looking at her with the eyes of a whelping. Our so-called friends and my mind-opening education would no longer be a bond for us. We were now on equal ground as far as I was concerned, and that meant some changes—she would have to give a bit on her proselytizing, I would have to be less reactionary (or perhaps less overreactionary), but we could work it out. All the nonsense and futility I had endured over the last year was for naught, but I still wanted her. How to salvage the relationship, how to find new connections, how to move to the next phase of my life but hang on to her, how to keep my hooks in this knockout babe—those questions loomed large.

Those questions would be answered that very evening. It was to be the last party of the school year. The significance of this was lessened by the fact that it was also the first party of the summer. The night was fresh and warm and filled with the anticipation of a carefree summer. No school to fret over, and more importantly, no mold of any kind to fit into. I was now thoroughly pose-proof. The rain had blanketed the city in glittery aurora and I was foolishly optimistic despite all my experiences.

Under a shared umbrella, I stared at Naomi. After all these months I was still overcome by her beauty. Her lips, even with no lipstick, seemed to glisten. Her skin was silken and perfectly toned. The contact of our hands on the umbrella handle and the radiant warmth of her shoulder pressed against mine could nearly burst my heart in the same way she could before we were even a couple and she was still only a fantasy. The whole scene—the new lifestyle, the change in major, the rift with the family, the noble poverty—was down the toilet now, except for Naomi. I vowed to work it out with her no matter what happened. As long as she would have me, I would figure out a way to keep us together. Overheated romantic notions of a mature, long-lasting relationship, in place of the mentor/disciple silliness, constituted my new vision. It might take some time. It certainly wouldn't be easy. But through perseverance, we would gain respect for each other deeper than just the lust and novelty we had shared so far. After that, who knows where life would lead?

The party itself moved from tiresome to maddening. It was the same old crowd, the group that I never really liked but tolerated for philosophical reasons, as it were. Now they were simply shallow and hopeless. Doomed, all of 'em; creatures of severely limited duration. I crossed Julian's path and paid him for my term paper. His unrelentingly indignant expression relaxed into a greedy smile as he pocketed the bills, then quickly reverted. Before I could make my exit he started in about some banal cause he had adopted that was becoming...

"...the single greatest issue confronting the planet. The globally aware agree that the events unfolding speak to the essence of the soul of the human race. From the outcome we will learn whether that soul is compassionate or decadent."

I had no idea what the cause was even though he had mentioned it thirty seconds earlier. I paid attention to Julian long enough to determine if what he said had any relevance to reality, or me in particular. If not, I purged the words from memory after about twenty seconds. In fact, with each succeeding conversation the persistence of his words grew shorter.

Suddenly a burnt-out, pot-head character I'd never seen before interrupted to ask if we had seen Doobie or not. He seemed to be paralyzed by our negative response, as if the fact we didn't know Doobie's whereabouts meant he would have to reevaluate existence from scratch. Having recently done that I had pity on him, especially considering he was clearly not up to dealing with any sort of mental activity, never mind metaphysical analysis.

"He'll probably be around soon," I said, which appeared to cheer him up. "Are you a friend of his?" I thought the simple question might kickstart his neurons.

"Oh, yeah, man. We've known each other since grade school. See, I'm, like, a writer—a monthly column for a hemp newsletter. Doobie is, like, our official bong tester, you know. I mean, he gives all the new bong designs the thumbs up or thumbs down, you know, like a movie review." He gave a friendly heh-heh. "See, I got some new equipment." He produced a contraption that, while resembling a bong in shape, also could have passed for a high-tech obelisk from a science fiction prop department.

"It's carbon fiber, with titanium fixtures and, check this out, a digital temperature gauge. Cool, huh? They're trying to sell them through Sharper

Image and Neiman Marcus, but no luck yet. If Doobie gives it a good review, it'll be a righteous bonus."

A statement stunning in its absurdity, yes, but something else impressed me.

"How old are you?" I asked.

"Twenty-three, man." That answer may have taxed his cognitive faculties a little too heavily and he moved off.

"Did you hear that?" I said to Julian.

"Hear what?"

Doobie arrived and met up with the hemp man so they could exchange the perfunctory "hey mans" and "alrights" and "rockin', dudes."

"Doobie's in his early twenties?" I continued in disbelief.

"So?"

"Duh. That means he was born in, what, the seventies. He was never in 'Nam."

"Look, that war has had a big effect on everyone in this society not just the people who were there," Julian explained. "Maybe he's just internalized all his guilt over the wars of oppression fought by this country. Like you, you probably still have unresolved issues over the Korean War. I mean, emotionally."

That remark was not eligible for purging. I turned to ice.

"I'm not Korean. I'm American. I was born in Grosse Pointe."

"Well, you were once, like, a generation ago."

"I'll be twenty-two next month."

It must have been I was speaking louder and more forcefully than I should have been because Naomi appeared out of nowhere and pulled me aside.

"You're doing it again. Why are you being so hostile? He's on your side you know."

I swore an oath, "Shit. Pure shit. Did you hear that shit? What kind of shit was that? Miserable little shit-eating weasel." I believe those were the only five times I ever swore in front of Naomi. From that she should have inferred how furious I was. She didn't; she just gave me the you're-being-too-reactionary look.

"He was trying to be sympathetic. Look, these people aren't the same as your old friends. You don't have to be hypersensitive with them."

"They're exactly the same! They say it with different motivation, but they still only see the stereotype. No different. That's what makes me angry! I thought they were different. This is such shit." OK, six times.

"You still don't understand do you?"

She didn't know when to stop. It was like talking to granite. Exquisitely sculptured, but still granite.

"Don't understand what?" I contested. "Maybe you're the one who doesn't understand. Maybe I'm finally starting to see things clearly."

"Then maybe it's best we end this."

"What do you mean?"

"I mean end us. I mean break up."

"You're breaking up with me?" This was working out well for me. Having vowed earlier that evening to keep her no matter what, I had now lost her in the course of about three minutes. Astounding, isn't it, my ability to achieve the exact opposite of my stated goals with such consummate efficiency?

"It's him, isn't it?" I was speaking of the shit-eating weasel. "I knew it. You've got something going with him. Isn't that just perfect shit." Eight. Damn.

"No, it's not him. I don't have anything going with anyone."

"So you're breaking up with me because I don't like your friends."

"Please don't trivialize our differences. Besides," she sighed sympathetically, "I've been meaning to tell you, I'm transferring to Arizona State for my graduate school."

My jaw turned to jelly. "What? When did you decide this?"

"Well, you know, my parents live near Tempe. It'll be cheaper if I go there. I'd like to stay in Ann Arbor, but I have to be realistic. I can't afford this school on my own. So, you see, it's just as well..."

I don't know if you have ever had an ice water enema—of course you haven't, no one has—but if you can imagine the sensation you have a good feel for my state of mind at that instant. When one is on the receiving end of an ice water enema, one is disinclined to listen attentively to the confessions of others. I don't even know if I stood there long enough for her to finish. I was outta there, running again.

TWENTY SIX

It was a good ten or fifteen seconds, or maybe minutes, or maybe hours, before the enema effect subsided. I was flying through the streets, the rain was needling into my skin like a swarm of killer bees, but I was not about to slow down.

Doobie was to be expected. He was so drug-addled that it was no surprise that his reality was fantasy and vice versa. Julian I could deal with. Because he prided himself on being so progressive I thought he would be the last one to indulge a racial stereotype despite his thoroughly distasteful personality. So firmly planted was his political correctness that I didn't expect that kind of comment from him. On the other hand, the guy was an asshole. So go figure.

But Naomi hit hard. The one thing that I was going to salvage from my ruinous adventure in self-discovery was rife with mendacity. Like the others, she was a pose, albeit a magnificently beautiful pose. All I needed was to find out that Odium was a CPA to make the sketch complete. Now all was lost. How did I manage that? The past hour had been a microcosm of the whole year; I went from certainty to squat before I knew what hit me.

The fact is, I thought my life had changed, but it was no different. I thought I was new and improved but I was simply repackaged. I thought I was nourishing my spirit, but it was all junk food.

Then I saw a sight that sent me reeling, literally. I staggered and stumbled through the mud for a good fifteen yards, looking like the second coming of Buster Keaton, but I didn't fall. I took a short moment to congratulate myself on this feat of dexterity, then rubbed my eyes and verified that what I saw was not a hallucination.

My professor, Prof. SLIME, the one to whom I had given a purchased term paper, the one who had been at the restaurant in my naked dream, was walking from car to house with a girl on his arm. They stopped before entering to share a nice long kiss, then went in without breaking their embrace. The girl was Toni with an i.

K.J.

I had to find K.J. I could talk to him. He would understand. I would confess and he would give me sanction.

I found the hidden spare key outside his door and let myself in. As I entered I took notice of the time. 3 AM. Since my enema, I had been running for over an hour. Briefly, I stood amazed at my own detachment from the universe, then I burst into his bedroom. Even though I was gulping air and panting from exhaustion, I was so wound up that I had to pace back and forth at the foot of his bed like super-caffeinated speed freak.

"She broke up with me! Can you believe that? She dumped me! I've been dumped! After all that she...Hey! Wake up!"

"Uh...Uh...Alex," he slurred.

"Are you listening?"

"There's no birds."

He had me there. "What are you talking about?"

"There's no birds. The birds aren't singing. You're soaking wet. It's three in the morning."

"Never mind about birds. Are you paying attention?" I ranted.

"Wha...When did you get here?"

"Naomi broke up with me."

"Oh." He sat up and shook himself awake. "Sit down. No, not on the bed. I have no desire to sleep in your wet spot."

"Can you believe that? After all that talk about freedom and rebellion, she leaves me 'cause she can't live without her parents. But it's no problem for me, is it? Feh!"

"Did you say feh?"

"Am I the biggest schmuck that ever lived?"

"Yes, of course you are. You are the biggest schmuck that ever lived. Although technically, I think you're a schlemiel. But that's not important right now. Take it from me, do what any self-respecting male would do in similar circumstances—deem the woman to be a psycho-bitch and move on."

"They're all like that. Posers. The whole lot of 'em. They think they're so elite and non-conformist and superior. They're just as full of it as everyone else. But who am I to complain—the biggest dork that ever lived."

"That's schmuck. The biggest schmuck that ever lived. Don't confuse me."

"I should have seen it coming. How stupid and naive can I be? I was doomed from the start, like some sickening Greek tragedy. The whole thing was doomed. Just totally doomed."

"Yes, yes, you were a doomed schmuck. Whatever. Listen; let me ask you a question. It might be kind of personal. You think Naomi might go out with me?"

Finally I stopped—stopped pacing, stopped panting, stopped self-pitying. I should have seen that coming. "What a dick."

"Feh."

APPLE PIE

TWENTY SEVEN

So there you are. Or rather, here I am. Summer is over, and, like I've said, I'm not going back to school. I'm officially a college drop out, with roughly seven-eighths of an engineering degree and one eighth of a philosophy degree. It's a strange sensation, seeing the waves of students return to school, buy books, fret over their classes, and me on the sidelines for the first time since before kindergarten. Nevertheless, I have achieved a certain acceptance of my position.

After closing at the restaurant one night we were all sitting around—me, K.J., a bunch of other the other waiters (not Naomi, she was gone by then) counting up our tips and having a beer to unwind. One of the waitresses mentioned that she'd heard I hadn't registered for the current semester and wondered how come. Given that it's taken me a whole book to explain it to you, I didn't quite have an easy answer, but I did manage to ramble out a short, somewhat dreamy summary.

"For so long in my life I followed a set path that was sure to lead me to security and stability. Then I chucked it all away to follow my heart and pursue my passion. Only it didn't turn out like it was supposed to and I was no better off than before, so I ended up without either life. What do you call someone like that?"

It's hard to imagine that such babble was perceived as an answer to the question. I thought, surely they must think me less than sober. There was a concerted pause, and then the answer came from everyone in unison. "A waiter."

And a bad one at that. I'm still a bad waiter to this day, only now I'm a bad waiter full time.

But back to the point: Why? No, not why am I a waiter. The metaphysical, write-a-book-about-it Why. Why did the last year of my life occur like it did? (Actually, they're the same question if you think really hard about it, but don't bother.) Not to romanticize the scene too much, but I still tend to fall back on fate and Greek tragedy for an explanation. There must be some aspect of my personality, some tragic flaw, which brought on that upheaval. If I could discover and clearly identify it, I could, if not overcome it, at least be prepared for subsequent upheavals.

Initially I thought it was my repressed nature. If I had stood up to my father and family earlier in life would I have had all this sorted out by now? The younger you screw up, the better. I never would have felt the need to break out and rebel by glomming onto a pack of abject wastrels and I would have saved myself the elevated level of schmuckhood I now possess.

But that begs the question: Where would I be if, at some young age, I took up that sort of cavalier and wonton attitude? I may have ended up a long-term member of Naomi's crowd, never able to see the pomposity and phoniness having never experienced another way. Conflicting desires allow you to see the falsehoods in each other—now that's deep philosophy.

Taken a step further (and I feel I must—sorry), what was it about these conflicting desires that rendered them false? Answer: they weren't mine to begin with. I started off with the Old Man's desire. I followed that path though duty and inertia until I saw the little girl who could spell. Thus, I was vulnerable to the opposite, believing the opposite must be the best way since I despised everything I was. I thought I had found the answer mostly because I wanted to so bad. And sex, of course. But it was really no different. It was someone else's desire—Naomi's for a worshiping disciple to be exact—so it too was lost. I traded my hard-working Asian cliche for a neo-bohemian free-spirit cliche. All along the truth was—and still is—that I don't really even know what my desires are. The cliches were just the easy way out.

I think. Maybe. It's the best I've come up with so far. If you feel as though you were misled into thinking there was going to be some pot-of-gold eternal truth at the end of this, my apologies. But you can't feel as disappointed as I do having discovered the most meaningful lesson that came from all the pain and chaos of the last year is simply Know Thyself.

Anyway, as I mentioned at the outset, there is one thing I know for sure, but first, a bit of Where Are They Now.

I never laid eyes on Naomi again. She had resigned from work the morning after the fateful enema night, before my next shift. I knew this because her name was erased from the schedule the next time I went in to work. No note. No call. No contact. Dust in the wind.

I periodically notice Doobie in his enigmatic wanderings. I've never approached him but we've made eye contact. He reacts with uncertain recognition; he should know me but from where? He's changed his look from straight green khaki to camouflage fatigues. I'm not sure what meaning to assign to that.

Julian never made it back to the rainforest. I saw him once, posting fliers for some unspeakably bad local rock band, possibly Neo-Techno-Goth-Industrial. No doubt he feels as though he is participating in some important cultural movement or something. I still hate the little shit-eating weasel.

I understand Ronnie moved to Hawaii, where he plans to make it legal with Garland.

Odium was the worst. She stalked me. It started with little encounters that could be passed off as innocent coincidence. She would happen to appear where I happened to be, giving me that empty stare of hers. I tried to make conversation, if you can call stream of consciousness non-sequitors in response to simple questions a conversation, which just encouraged her. Then it started to get annoying. I tried to ignore her, but I began getting phone calls with no one on the other end. Once I realized what was going on I stopped saying "Hello" and asked, "Who is this?"

"Odium."

I'd just hang-up. Then the stalking began in earnest. She started following me around. I kept telling her to stop, but she paid no attention. Once she even followed me to the restaurant and sat in the corner like a gargoyle while I worked my shift. That took some explanation to the diners, especially the out-of-towners who had mistakenly hung their coats on her. She was banned from the restaurant under threat of legal action and I moved into a new apartment. As a result, I haven't seen her since, except on the cover of a local radical tabloid, *The Ann Arbor Agenda*, which hailed the onset of the Poetic Age of Odium.

The Dweebs; remember them? I saw them on graduation day in their caps and gowns. Useless seemed particularly pleased since his cap protected him from a noogie assault. I congratulated them and we briefly made some minor small talk. They were all going to work for real career type companies, making real money type salaries. We made polite but groundless vows to keep in touch. They even made it clear that I was still welcome back with them. Thanks, but I don't think so. It did occur to me that, despite their grotesque existence, they were much better friends than I had given them credit for. Much better friends than I had abandoned them for. But they're still dweebs, and I'm not.

K.J. is still my best friend and MFG is still high on my priority list. He graduated too; English major. He's working for a comic book publisher, writing superhero stories. Oh, sorry, not comic books—Graphic Novels. It's funny how often I make that mistake in his presence. Truthfully, he's quite lucky. He's the only one I know with an English degree that actually gets paid to write.

The thing about K.J. is he saw the whole thing for what it was. Through all my hapless stupidity that year, he knew what I was getting myself into and setting myself up for. I know this only now, as I think back to his tolerant reactions and sympathetic facetiousness. He said nothing while it was happening and was correct to do so. It's not like anything short of an ice water enema was going to wake me up. Like everything else, we don't discuss it; it's just understood.

Family-wise, nothing's really changed. The Old Man and I aren't talking. George is delighted to be back in a state of grace and running the company that was supposed to be for Sarah and me. He's close to achieving his true desire, not actually working but having everyone believe he's earning every cent. The guy's a real piece of work.

The rift between the Old Man and me bothers Mom a lot. She's always trying to reconcile us, subtly and quietly of course. Donna Reed/June Cleaver/Carol Brady could do no less. But the whole thing's beginning to look like a lost cause and I think she's coming to accept that the Old Man and me will never be like family. So I talk to her regularly and we go out to lunch or dinner now and then to maintain contact. The only part of the whole mess that still makes me uncomfortable is that it causes Mom distress.

Which brings me to my favorite subject: Me.

As I pointed out before, I'm now a full-time bad waiter. And I've picked up a second job part-time at the big Barnes and Noble bookstore; helps make ends meet and I get inexpensive reading material. I don't hide my country music CDs anymore. I haven't got a steady girlfriend though I do spend a lot of time socializing with my friends and acquaintances. It may sound rather empty and, dare I say it, prosaic, but actually it's kind of nice. I have my whole life to re-enter the rat race; for now I'll let it slide. A little stretch of the undirected time may give me the freedom to sort out my desires before I make another stupid commitment. Plus, it gives you time to write a book.

TWENTY EIGHT

And now we have come full circle to what I know for sure.

I was in Sweetwater Cafe killing time over a Mocha-chino when in walks just about the most beautiful woman I have ever seen. I know you've heard that before about a certain blonde, but this one came from another direction. Where Naomi was auspicious and ethereal, this woman was darkly glamorous and sultry. And quite Asian. Korean, as it turned out. It was Sarah. She looked so stunning that I felt my signature tight pain in the abdomen when our eyes met. She practically cat-walked over to my table with this gawky looking Korean geek in tow.

"Hello Alex."

"Uh, Sarah. How are you?"

"May we join you?"

"Uh, of course."

She then spoke to the geek as if he were a pet. "Why don't you get us a couple of coffees?"

"OK," said the geek.

"I'll have a Vanilla Cinnamon," she said to the geek, as if he would be punished if he didn't get it right.

"OK."

"Alex do you want another?" she asked.

"Yeah. Mocha-chino."

"And a Mocha-chino for Alex."

"OK."

The geek slouched off to stand in line. A remarkable performance considering her past. She took the chair directly across from me as I looked on in disbelieving awe. Could this really be Sarah? Dull, plain, boring, little Sarah? Just enough make-up, invisibly applied; flat Asian hair all permed and wild looking; seductive, slightly devilish grin, form-fitting halter-top—with a navel ring. And looking me straight in the eye while confidently ordering around some helpless sap. Whoa.

"I'm surprised you even want to speak to me after the way I treated you. You know, I didn't really want to hurt you," I offered.

"You wouldn't know what you wanted," she responded, quickly and correctly. "Sorry. That was mean. I'm not upset. I was for a while, but then I realized I set myself up for it being such a meek little mouse."

APPLE PIE

She laughed a frighteningly cosmopolitan laugh, the laugh of the victorious when confronted with the absurd hopes of the defeated.

"I decided not to let people take advantage of me so much; to look out for myself more. So I suppose, in a way, it was good."

"Whatever you did, it worked. You look incredible, just incredible. An incredible transformation. Really...Really...uh, really pretty." That's me, Joe Smooth.

"Thank you," she said with immeasurable indifference. "I heard about you and your father. It caused an awful lot of gossip in the Korean community."

"No doubt. I'm such a terrible person to bring that shame on my family."

"So what are you going to do now? Go back to school?"

"Can't afford to. Don't want to. Don't know. Don't even care. I'm just gonna cruise for a while, I guess."

Again the laugh, and preening shake of hair as a preface to a come-hither sort of look that could melt tungsten. I was not worthy of this girl anymore. Never was, really. No way. Not in a million years. Not that that stopped me.

"Are you serious with this guy?" I asked, indicating the geek who was struggling to explain his order to the coffee-dude.

She just gave me an as-if look.

I went for it. "I don't suppose you'd like to get together again. You know, just to see if the old spark is still there."

The as-if look heightened. "I don't think so. After you, I don't think I'd ever go out with another American."

Yup, that's it. American. For sure.

The End